Fractured

By Ryan Mayers

PublishAmerica

Baltimore

First printing

ISBN: 1-4137-0309-7
PUBLISHED BY PUBLISHAMERICA, LLLP
www.publishamerica.com
Baltimore

Printed in the United States of America

Prologue

"Are you sure you feel up to this?"

"Yea. It needs to be done, right?"

"Yep." He shifted in his seat. "Any time you're ready, ok?"

"Ayuh. Let me just get myself settled here."

"That's ok."

I lay back in the bed, thinking back over all that had happened. The last few days were a blur, but this was important. I had to get this right. Debriefings were bad enough under normal conditions; when you were stuck in a hospital bed they were far worse. I looked down to where my feet were pushing up the blanket, little tents where my toes poked up, reflected on how often I had been in this same building in the last few days, and then glanced at the ground, at where the body had fallen, already knowing but still feeling relieved to see that there was no sign of what had happened. The last thing I needed was another reminder of death.

The cop in the chair had brought a tape recorder (one of those off brand types you could buy at convenience stores the world over for less than twenty dollars... they had really laid down some serious cash for that machine... I was actually surprised it didn't explode the second he took it out of the package... darned cheap government) which he had plugged in just above the cord for the bed. As he popped a tape in, I looked in his face and saw a twinge of excitement. He knew something big had happened and I was the only one who could shed any serious light on it. Seven deaths in the last few days, an explosion, a shoot out, a decapitation... It was enough to make anyone a little on edge. I took a deep breath, and then nodded at the cop. He nodded back and pressed the record button. The little red light came on, reminding me of a recurring nightmare I had had as a kid. There was this monster that came out of my closet at night and ate me, but he didn't do it all at once. He liked to nibble on my toes, then work his way up my legs, savoring each and every bite. I usually woke up before he got past my kneecap. Anyway, he had red eyes. I shook my head. This was no time for stupid thoughts that like that. No, this was the time for remembering. This was the time to begin.

I. The King's Men

The house was squat, with a thatched roof and what looked almost like adobe walls. Everything about it was rounded, reminding me oddly of the papier-mache masks I used to make as a kid. We would mix glue and water and then dip strips of newspaper into the goop and layer them over a balloon. Then, when they dried, we would pop the balloon and cut the shell in half. Man, I can remember decorating those things for hours. Ahh, the simplicities of youth. What I wouldn't give for those now....

There were tufts of straw sticking out from various places on the house, as though some crazed builder had gotten a little impatient with the overall progress of the building and decided to throw random bunches of hay in the general direction of the roof (and not doing a very good job of that, either), and the window shades were painted a light green reminiscent of the grass I'm always having to cut in the summer. Stupid grass. They can put a man on the moon, but they can't teach my grass to just stop growing. Anyway, the lights were off and the shades were drawn, giving the house an abandoned feel. Despite that, we snuck up on the house as quiet as we could. The last thing in the world we wanted was to wake up the inhuman monster within. Well, that's actually the wrong way to say it. We snuck up so as not to alert the monster known as Mr. Waddles.

First, a word of explanation. My name is John Monroe, although everyone calls me Cap. I'm a detective in the King's Men, the Breco police. See, what you know as fairy tales and nursery rhymes come from a place called Breco and they're generally propaganda stories aimed at instilling morals in the minds of the citizens of our fair country. The problem is that most of them are a load of crap.

Take, for instance, the tale of Old Mother Hubbard. Yea, her cupboard was bare, but they never tell you the reason. You wanna know why? It's because sweet little Old Mother Hubbard was running a sweet little old brothel from out of her house. We were forced to close her down, and Johnson wrote that little tale as a way of letting everyone know what happens if you break the law (you go hungry, apparently... I never said Johnson was too good with the words...). I personally find the whole thing a bit fluffy, especially since we actually took the Old Mother after she tried to swallow half an ounce of pure uncut heroin and puked all over the place. It was smellier than week old cheese, and not the refrigerated kind.

Anyway, back to my main point. I work for the King's Men. The King's Men were formed many, many years ago when the King decided that his subjects needed to learn to fear the law. No more could there be pure anarchy on the streets. So, we were formed. When we started, most of our cases were easy. There'd usually be a lost and found case every week, the occasional disappearance. As time went on, though, we got caught up in that seemingly unexplainable growth that all cities inevitably undergo. I don't mean expansion, although that might have had something to do with it. I mean the growth of shadiness. Of crime, of violence. Of disrespect and hatred. Somewhere along the line we had become a city that had to worry about murder, rape, drugs, and hate, all those things we used to think we were, well, nigh invincible against. What made it worse was that the crimes just kept getting more heinous. This particular case, in fact, was probably the worst I'd ever seen.

It all started about three weeks ago, when the little piggy who went to the market didn't come home. His family (now down to nine little piggies all cowering in the corner from fear) reported him missing right away, but we couldn't do anything. You have to be missing for twenty-four hours before anything can be done, so it really wasn't our fault. After the time had passed, we went out looking, but we just couldn't find anything. We told the pigs we'd keep it up, but missing persons cases (or, in this case, missing pig cases) aren't all that high on the priority sheet, and so we didn't try very hard. It was a bad turn of luck, though, because within the next two weeks every single one of the little pigs (save the last one, who ran home screaming 'wee, wee, wee', apparently from fright) disappeared.

We tried to track them down, but had no luck. All we were able to find was traces of blood at a few of the scenes, and so we were prepared for the worst. The first crack in the case came when we found a message, scrawled in some clumpy redness that we almost immediately identified as blood. The problem was that no one could actually read it. We puzzled over that message for hours, trying to make it say things in English, in French, in German, in various 'linguas otras', and even in signs, but blood can be a very uncooperative witness, and this particular sample had apparently learned a thing or two about keeping its mouth shut. That's when Jack Horner suddenly got the bright idea of using a mirror. He said that he thought of it because the pictures of the scene showed a broken mirror in front of the message, and that he was suddenly hit with the thought that maybe the mirror hadn't been broken when the message was scrawled. We tried it and he was right, of course.

The message was two words, scrawled nearly incomprehensibly: bacon square. If it weren't for the fact that this was something very bad (that is, if the message weren't scrawled in blood like some sort of demented blood pact between kids), I would have laughed. It sounded so dumb. Bacon square. Of course, then Horner decided that the e in square was a little too muddled for his tastes, and was able to pull out a d, making it squared. Bacon squared. What would that entail? We decided that bacon in the one sense could be a pig, and thus this was some sort of pig on pig violence and not an interspecies hate crime. That was a relief since we were already dealing with a gang of apes that had been pulled in after beating an old orangutan. They said he was making faces at them, and he said that's what his face always looked like. Very ugly case. Anyway, the other bacon puzzled us for a while.

Cops are typically called pigs, but we hadn't had a pig cop on the force since that friggin' Micke "Oink" Strewlan went crazy and tried to kill one of the butchers down on Main. That was right after the bill outlawing pork products was passed, and the butchers in the area weren't very happy about it. This particular one had been quite verbal in his anger, even going so far as to insinuate that pigs shouldn't have the right to vote, let alone live among humans. I guess one day Micke just flipped his lid and he attacked the guy with a knife. Managed to sink it between the guy's shoulder blades before he was pulled off. Apparently he was screaming out the names of various pork products as he did it. He had just reached pork chops when they finally wrestled him off. The whole thing was a big stink, the papers picked it up, and in the end Micke went to jail for a long time, narrowly avoiding the death penalty when the butcher miraculously recovered. Thinking of Micke, however, made me think of butchers, and I realized that bacon could stand for someone of that particular profession (at least in a pig's mind), thus making our guy a pig butcher. Everyone liked that idea, and we looked it up, finding that there was only one in the entire Breco area, and that was Mr. Waddles.

We brought him in and asked him all sorts of questions. Why would we find a bloody message pointing to you? Do you know where the pigs are? What the heck is that smell? And so on. The smell turned out to be Mr. Waddles getting a little hot under the collar from the bright lights we were using in the interrogation room. We had to get him outside so he could cool off. Darn room smelled like ham for days. He had answers for all our questions, though, and most of them were really good, too (he was a little uncooperative at first and we had to threaten him with a trip to the drunk tank... those drunks will eat anything... he talked after that). In the end we were forced to let him go since we didn't really have anything on him, but something just didn't feel right about the whole thing.

And so we set up a watch on Mr. Waddles' house. The first few days were okay, nothing out of the ordinary, but before too long he started to act a little funny. It wasn't anything any of us could verbalize, but something about the way he was acting was, well, a little off. So, we started to lower the net. We took pictures of him at the butcher shop, and we used directional mics and the like to listen to him at home. It was at work when we finally caught him. We were taking pictures from across the street when a man in a black trench coat walked in and nodded to Mr. Waddles, who immediately came over and shut his door, swinging the "Open" sign around so it read "Closed" (both words drawn to look like bloody intestines shaped into letters). We trained all our mics and cameras on the store, and caught just enough of the conversation to find out that the man in the coat wanted a "fresh shipment" in "three days". But a shipment of what? It didn't matter, we decided, because the circumstances seemed enough to get us a search warrant, and we began planning the attack on the house itself.

And that's where things stood. We were sneaking up on Mr. Waddles' house to try and catch him and his shipment before they both left in the morning. Dumpty, my partner, reached the squat little house first and turned to look at the rest of us. I was on my way up when I saw the door behind Dumpty opening, slowly and silently. Apparently someone knew we were coming. I motioned frantically to him to turn around, but the dimwitted fool didn't get it. He just waved back with a big smile on his face. When I pointed at the door he just nodded and motioned that he was going to open it. Before anyone knew what was happening, Mr. Waddles shot out from between Dumpty's legs and sprinted off down the road. We immediately took off after him, some in cars and some on foot.

Mr. Waddles veered off to the left and ducked under a low-lying branch. Dumpty reached it first and jumped over. I was right behind and followed his lead. Ahead I could vaguely see Dumpty, an outline in the fading moonlight, come to a dead standstill and look around. Mr. Waddles, apparently, was nowhere to be found.

He listened hard and must have heard something off to the right, 'cause that's where he started running. I reached the clearing and stopped to look around. There were trees encircling this little bit of open land, and three paths meandered off into the rest of the forest: the one I had just come off, the one Dumpty had just run down, and the one directly in front of me.

I was about to go for the one in front of me when I heard a sneeze from behind me. I turned, saw nothing, and then tried looking below the tree line. There, pressed up against the trunk of the tree, was a pair of pink, stocky legs. I pulled my gun and trained it on the figure I knew was behind the leaves.

"Come on out, Waddles, I got you covered." The figure didn't move, and I slowly moved forward. As nice as the freakin pigs can be, they don't seem to have any compunction against knifing someone when they get mad, and in this particular case I thought it to be quite likely that there was a knife waiting for me. I reached the tree and said it again. "Come on, man. I don't want to have to shoot you. Just come out peacefully and we'll talk about this."

Still, the figure didn't move, so I got down on my knees and, keeping the gun firmly in one hand, reached out and grabbed one of the feet under the tree, meaning to pull Waddles out forcefully. The foot didn't want to come, though. No matter how hard I pulled, it wouldn't move away from the tree. Finally, I stood back up and pulled some branches away to allow me to see.

The figure behind the tree was definitely not Mr. Waddles. The odds are that the figure was, at one time, the pig who went to market (poor little guy was really fat, and the face I was looking into had jowls to rival those of Mr. Grimley, my 300 pound high school principal from back in the day), but now the word pig didn't really see to fit. Never again would he get the chance to say 'wee'. His feet were intact, as were his hands and his head, but the rest was picked clean, nothing but a skeleton.

I almost puked, especially when I saw the eyes, glazed in red, seemingly staring right into mine. I stumbled away, letting go of the branches, and leaned over near the middle of the circle to let my lunch (which didn't even taste so good going down) come back out. That's about when I noticed the stains on the ground.

The entire circle was covered in a reddish, iron smelling stickiness that was instantly identifiable. I tried hard to swallow the bile that had so readily risen into my throat. This was the scene of a massacre. There was way too much blood here for just the one poor pig behind me, and I had a sudden flash of nine separate sets of eyes staring out at me.

That's when I remembered the sneeze I had heard. I turned quickly, and just in time. Mr. Waddles had snuck up behind me and had a knife raised above his head, about to lower it into my back. I pointed the gun at him and he froze.

"Now, Waddles," I managed to choke out, my eyes strenuously avoiding the tree with the dead pig tied to it. "You can do that if you really want to, but I promise you I'll get off one shot. And right now," I said, as I aimed the gun at his crotch, "you definitely don't want that." Mr. Waddles' eyes were blazing, red fire in a black hearth. It was a standoff of sorts. I almost expected a western twang and a tumbleweed to come rolling between us. He seemed to be running through his options. Finally, after what seemed like hours and hours, he lowered the knife and sighed, in a resigned way.

He looked into my eyes and I caught my breath. They say the eyes are the window into the soul, and if that's true then this pig's soul was the absolute picture of tormented hell. It hurt me just to look at him, and so I started to turn my eyes away.

Apparently that's what he was waiting for, because as soon as my glance wavered he brought the knife back up and tried to put it into his own throat. I jerked my arm out, grabbed his stubby little forearm and tugged back, only to have my hand slide right off. He had apparently greased himself up before leaving the house, because try as I might I couldn't hold his freakin arm. He looked at me again, his murderous rage seemingly emanating off his skin, and slowly brought the knife to his throat again.

"I can't let you take me in." He started to push it in, and I shot him in the leg. The sound was deafening in the small place, but it did the trick. He dropped the knife and started swearing while simultaneously grabbing his leg and trying to keep his balance.

I put my arms under his and carried him back to the house like a bag of potatoes. After depositing him in a chair at the kitchen table, I sat next to him and started rubbing my temples. "I want a friggin doctor!" He slammed his fist down on the table. "I got my rights too, ya know."

"Hey, shut up, ok? I gotta headache."

"Oh, la-di-frikkin-da. I got a friggin bullet through my leg, and you're complaining about a headache. Well, excuse me if I don't join you in your weeping."

I aimed my gun at his head. "Look, Waddles. I really am a nice guy, but these headaches... They make me do things I regret later." I looked into his eyes, trying to fight the evil I saw there. "Capiche?"

He just glared back at me, but he stopped talking, so I think he capiched just fine. I stood and motioned Officer Swanson over. "Have you heard from Dumpty?"

"Nope. Sorry Cap."

I swore under my breath, then left Waddles under the watchful eyes of Swanson and started looking for Dumpty. He wasn't in the living room, the bathroom, the bedroom, the yard... He was just nowhere to be found, even though everyone else had returned. That was kinda weird, but there was nothing I could do about it, so I reluctantly went back and sat down to ask Waddles some questions.

See, Dumpty had been my partner for many, many years, and I didn't feel right asking this monster any questions without him. Unfortunately, the ambulance would be here soon to take him away, and so I had no choice. Waddles was staring off into space, bobbing his head to some beat only he could hear. I waited until he looked at me and started in.

"Ok, Waddles. First off, where are they?"

"Who?"

"Cut the crap, alright? I don't have time for this."

"Oh, I think you have more time than you think."

"What's that supposed to mean?" No answer. I stood. "I said what's that supposed to mean?"

"Bite me."

I thought it over and decided against it. "Sorry, man. I don't know where you been."

"Your mom didn't seem to have a problem with it."

"Oh, that's it." I grabbed Waddles by the shoulders. "You listen to me you overgrown piece of ham. I've had enough of this. You will answer my questions and you will answer them now. Where are they?" He suddenly broke into a grin and cocked his head. "Well?"

Then he burped, a really noxious one that allowed me to make a pretty good guess at what he had eaten for any given meal in the last year or so. I let him go and he slumped into the chair.

"Guess, you dirty prig." I drew my gun again, but he just sneered at me. "You know, this is police brutality." He gestured at his leg, which looked oddly shredded in the harsh lights of the kitchen. His voice was calmer, although there was still a definite edge. I shook my head, clearing the thoughts away, and slowly put my gun away.

"Where are they?"

"Where are who?"

"Where are the pigs, you little freak?"

"Oh, I see how it is. Anyone who isn't like you is a freak. I love you, man. You're just making my case better."

"Look, shut the heck up about your 'case', and tell me what I want to know. Where are they?" He let go of his leg and looked me square in the face, leaning in to give it more emphasis.

"I don't know who you're talking about."

"I don't believe you."

"And I care so much about what you believe." He rolled his eyes.

"Listen to me, tubby." I stood and grabbed him by the shirt collar, slowly lifting him out of his seat until his face was right in front of mine. "I don't have time for this. All I care about is those little pigs, and if you don't tell me where they are then I swear to God that I'm gonna…" Johnson interrupted me.

"Oh crap." It was weak, nearly gurgled out, as though he was speaking through a veil of half digested food particles. "Hey Cap? I think you're gonna want to come look at this." I turned my face to look through the door to the garage, where Johnson was bent over a freezer. I regretfully put Waddles down and, nodding to Swanson to keep an eye on him again, made my way out the door and over to the freezer.

Johnson was looking paler than that stupid sheep of Bo Peep's and was struggling to keep his feet. I looked at him and he motioned with his head for me to look in the freezer, which I approached with a fair amount of trepidation. I'd already seen both a dismembered

15

body and the effects of a bullet at close range, so I wasn't looking forward to whatever this might turn out to be.

I reached the freezer and peered over the edge, then jumped back, feeling my own veil winding its way up my throat. There, in the bottom of the freezer, were nine little packages of bacon. They would be almost cute if I didn't know where they had come from.

I stumbled back, past the door, and bumped into the cabinet on the other side, which made me jump and, startled, move forward, only to get hit in the back by the opening doors. I turned around and saw, to my utter horror, shelf upon shelf of pork rinds. Salted, barbecued, salt and vinegar... Flavor upon flavor of fried pork skin.

I was feeling seriously ill now, and I turned my gaze away, looking through the open door into the kitchen and at Waddles, who had seen all that had taken place. He raised his eyebrows toward me and smiled a malicious little smile that reminded me oddly of some evil and malignant wolf. I had to get out of the house.

I ran through the kitchen into the dining room and left through the front door, finally losing it on the grass outside. Standing there with my hands on my knees, bent over, for a few minutes, I finally gained some composure, stood and looked back at the house. I was trying to steel my nerves enough to go back in when the ambulance pulled up. The medics jumped out and carried a stretcher into the house. Grateful for the reprieve, I walked over to my car and leaned on the hood, watching as the medics came out carrying the monster and slid him, quite easily, into the back of the ambulance. Johnson, who had drawn the short lot, hopped in the back to accompany the prisoner to the hospital.

I got in the passenger side of the car, with my feet hanging out the door, and grabbed the radio. "Dispatch," I sent out. "Dispatch, this is Cap. We need a crew out at 13 Snakeskin Street. It's..." I thought about what I was going to say. It's common knowledge that the media monitor the channel, and I wanted to keep them away as long as I could. "It's a pork fest out here."

I had just let go of the receiver when a call came back. "Cap? Cap this is Dispatch."

I lifted the receiver up again. "Yea Dispatch, this is Cap."

"There you are. Listen, you might want to get over to the GW Bridge. It's..." Her voice fell. "It's Dumpty." A thrill went through me. The voice on the other end was cracked with emotion, not something I was used to at all. It boded very badly for the situation. Dumpty? No. It couldn't be. Dumpty was my partner. Without him I was lost.

"Alright." I choked it out. Tonight was shaping up to be quite an interesting one. I got out and moved into the driver's seat, started the car, and headed off.

II. Humpty Dumpty

The GW Bridge spans Buckwalter Pond, which is right in the center of Maurice Krendall Park (named, oddly enough, for the man who single-handedly fought against the clean air initiative, and lost. It was supposed to be some sort of a snub, I think). I reached it in about three minutes, thinking the entire time of how this couldn't really be happening, of how he had run off by himself and if I had only yelled after him then he would still be here.

Of course, if I had yelled then we wouldn't have caught our man, but that was something I was willing to live with. Then I thought of his wife. Mrs. Dumpty was one of the nicest people I knew. Throughout the years I had worked with Dumpty, I couldn't remember a single time when her words were mean, or even edged. This was gonna kill her. I couldn't imagine what her grief would be like, much less how their kids would take it.

I could see where they were even before coming in sight of the bridge. The blackness of the night was broken by the blue flashes of the lights on the police cruisers, and by the garish white of a spotlight. Why they had that, I couldn't guess, but I knew that in just a few more seconds I would know.

I pulled up to the back of the pack and turned off the ignition. Sitting there, behind the wheel, I had a sudden urge to turn the car back on and just drive off. Head for someplace tropical, leave all this crap behind me. The more I thought about it, the better it seemed. My hand had actually made its way to the keys before I caught control of myself. I'm a cop. I've seen horrible things most people only dream about (or, at the very least, have nightmares about). I eat doughnuts. I should be able to handle anything.

With my new superhero outlook on life, I opened the door and climbed out. The smell hit me almost immediately, managing to knock all that newfound strength right outta me. It was as if someone had started cooking an omelet and then forgot about it. Burnt yolk. I felt my stomach trying to push some newly discovered bit of culinary goodness up my throat, but suppressed it and started off.

Walking towards the gaggle of people who were at the edge of the bridge, I noticed some of the cops were looking over the edge and some were looking away, struggling to keep their own stomachs under control. As I reached the group, I saw that Captain Stevenson was there, looking sadder than a kid whose favorite stuffed animal just got sucked up by the lawn mower. That was always a bad sign. When a big, important guy like Stevenson deemed it necessary to actually go to the scene of a tragedy, then you knew it had to be big. He saw me coming and his face, amazingly, grew even sadder. I went right to him.

"What happened?"

He pulled me away from the bridge. "Listen, son. I don't think you want to look over there. Deputy Dumpty... has had an accident." The words seemed to wrench something loose in him and he slumped his shoulders. I struggled against him, but he held me firm. "Did you hear what I just said?"

I stopped struggling and looked at him. "Captain, I heard you, and I understand what you're trying to do. But, you gotta see this from my perspective. He's my partner. I've worked with Humpty for a long time, and he's almost like family to me." The captain looked at me. I already knew what had happened, I thought, so I couldn't figure out why he wouldn't let me look. Then, in an instant, I knew. Humpty wasn't just dead, he was splattered.

I ducked under the captain's arm and ran to the edge. At this end of the bridge, there was a seven or eight foot stretch where the bridge passes about ten feet of ground before reaching the pond. It was here that Humpty had fallen off. Humpty had never been able to handle the gruesome stuff, and I had always made jokes about how thin skinned he was. I realized then how wrong I had been to do that.

The fall was little more than thirty feet at this point, but that had been enough. Humpty's shell was in a billion little pieces, and his insides were splattered all over. The side of the wall was soaked in a ten-foot radius from where he landed. Bushes lining the opposite side of the path reflected light dully off their new coating of egg white. There was a crumpled pile at the base of the bridge. A uniform, a large number of slightly off-white shards. It was, in all reality, almost as if a water balloon had exploded, only instead of being filled with water, it was filled with Dumpty parts. I retched, having already lost my dinner that night, and turned away disgusted.

The captain was behind me. "I tried to tell you."

"I know." I was trying not to lose it. This was too much for one night. My left hand was shaking and the world seemed to be getting darker by the second.

The captain looked over the side. "I don't think there's much use in trying to put him back together again. He's gone." He turned back to me.

"Do we know what happened?" I asked.

"Not yet," he replied. "The best we've been able to figure is that he fell from here." He pointed to the side of the bridge, where I could see a slight film of white powder apparently scraped from his side.

I looked at it, the truth dawning in my head. "Wait. If that's there, then he was pushed over." My revulsion at the sight quickly turned into anger. The captain looked at his feet.

"Yea... It would appear that Dumpty's great fall wasn't an accident. We were gonna try and find all the pieces, see if we couldn't at least put part of him back together, but..." He trailed off, then looked at me. "Monroe, Dumpty was killed." The word had the effect of a hammer on me, finally breaking through the stoic front I had projected and shattering me from the inside out. I remember feeling relief as the world suddenly turned as dark as the inside of a closet, only less musty.

* * *

Then, seemingly instantaneously, I was in a bed in the hospital. A worried nurse was looking over me, and in the background I could hear muzak. Something from the mid-eighties, but I couldn't quite place it, though the crappiness of it had a comforting effect on me. When she saw my eyes fluttering, the nurse gave a quick yelp and hurried out, giving me ample opportunity to admire, uh, the stitching on the back of her dress....

When she was gone, I began to look around. I was in a hospital room, that much was sure. I reached up and felt my head, then snaked a hand under the covers. After patting around quickly, I ascertained that everything seemed to be in the right place. I sat up and yawned. I felt fine. I tried to think of why I was in the hospital, and then everything came flooding back. Humpty was dead, there was a cannibal pig in the county jail, and I was stuck in a friggin' hospital, but at least I had a nurse with, um, a very well stitched uniform. Right then, the door opened and the captain walked in.

"Monroe." He nodded to me. I nodded back, but he took no notice. He paced over to the window on the far wall and looked out at the sunlit day. His hands were grasped behind his back, and I could tell from his demeanor that something was up. He drew in some breath and turned around.

"Monroe, do you know why you're here?"

"Not really."

"Ahh." He turned back around and spoke again. "You fainted on the GW Bridge last night." He let his breath out. "I assume you remember what happened?"

"Well, yea. Everything except the fainting, apparently."

"Ahh." He turned again. Humpty's death had apparently really affected him a lot. The captain seemed to have aged twenty years since I'd seen him last. His face was haggard and drawn, and I would be willing to swear that a whole new crop of the little gray hairs had found a home up top. "It's a weird one, John."

"What do you mean?"

"Well, you know that they just installed the video cameras on the GW." I did. I was instrumental in their installation, actually, insisting that they were the only way to catch the purse-snatcher who'd been running loose in the park. He liked the bridge, but so far we hadn't got him. I hadn't even thought of the cameras.

"Did you get the killer already?"

"See, that's the thing. We watched the video, and you can see Humpty being pushed off the bridge, and see him hitting the ground, but you can't see who it was that did it."

That was a little disturbing. Killers are bad enough in general, but when the killer is smart enough to avoid being seen by a camera... I sighed. "So, you're upset because you don't know who did it?"

"Well..." he started. The door opened then, though, so he didn't get to finish. Mrs. Dumpty came running in and stood over the bed. She'd quite obviously been crying.

"Oh John, he's dead!" Her voice rose to a shriek, and she started sobbing again. The captain looked at her and sighed. It was always hard....

"I know." I reached out my hands to hug her, and she leaned in.

"I think I'll go," said the captain, heading for the door.

"No you don't," said Mrs. Dumpty. "I want to talk to you." She walked over to him and they left the room. I watched them go and lay back. What a day....

* * *

They released me that afternoon. There really wasn't anything wrong with me; I was just a little overwhelmed. It felt good to be out in the open air again, even if only for the short stretch between the hospital doors and the garage. The captain had had one of the guys drive my car over for me, and it was easy to find.

I opened the door and climbed in, resting for a moment before starting the car up. Everything seemed different now. Sounds were magnified, sights were sharper. The groaning of the engine as it turned over seemed even more gravelly than usual, and as I watched the world became a myriad of different pictures. The tears came quickly, profusely, streaming down my face and onto the collar. I thought of

Dumpty. I thought of our past, of all the things I loved about him, and I just couldn't stop.

Eventually I settled down enough to grab hold of my emotions, and I dried my face on my sleeve. It felt good to let some of it out, but it was neither the time nor the place for a complete breakdown. I drove out of the garage and left the lot. My first stop was the grocery store, to pick up some milk and other essentials (also, truth be told, to show off my hospital bracelet and hope for some sympathy) and then I headed home.

I lived on the other side of town from Waddles, the cannibal pig, in a new apartment building built over the site of an old slum. I reflected as I waited for the elevator that would take me to my fifth floor apartment that I had done a lot in this town. The slum was shut down largely through my work. The elevator arrived and I stepped in.

The only other passenger was Miss Emily, from the sixth floor. She was carrying a laundry basket filled with clothes, which meant that she had come from the basement. I looked at her, and then shifted my gaze to the floor, blushing.

She too looked a little flustered, but that could have just been because some of her daintier laundry pieces were lying on top of the basket in plain view. Miss Emily was quite good looking, and, truth be told, I had a little thing for her. I had always suspected that she had a little thing for me, too, but both of us were too shy to ever try and make something come of it.

Now, however, she raised her head and looked right at me. "Are you ok?"

The words sounded so sweet coming from her lips. "Yea, I'm fine. I fainted. Pretty brave, huh?"

She laughed, a musical little giggle that made me somehow very, very happy. I felt like I was floating, and not just because the elevator was stopping. "Well, I can see why."

She turned her eyes to the front page of the newspaper that was lying to the side in her basket of clothes. There was a large picture of the Waddles house, and the headline screamed about cannibalism in suburbia. The second story on the cover was about Dumpty's untimely death.

"I read all about it," she said. "It sounds like you're a hero. You caught that disgusting Waddles. I always knew something was wrong with him." She tapped two fingers to her head and nodded gravely, but in a very cute way. The bell dinged for the fifth floor, and I regretfully stepped through the opening doors and off the elevator. Suddenly, seized with a boldness I didn't know I possessed, I put my hand in the closing doors and made them open again.

"Hey, why don't you come down for coffee sometime?"

She blushed and looked down. "Ok," she mumbled. She looked back up with a huge smile on her face. "When?"

I looked at my watch and thought about it. "Well, I should be back around nine, if you wanna come down then." She nodded.

"I think I'll do that. See you then, Officer." She winked as the doors closed between us. My heart, which had been trip hammering ever since my traitorous mouth uttered the words, suddenly took off soaring. I floated down the hall to my door, which I tried to open three times before remembering to unlock it, and then kept right on floating in, closing the door behind me. After putting the groceries down, I was confronted by an answering machine with twenty some odd messages.

I rubbed my eyes and pushed play, then went to the fridge and grabbed a bottle of orange juice while listening to the messages. Most of them were from friends and relatives who were worried. The story had been picked up across the kingdom, and everyone knew about it. The last message was from the captain, telling me that I shouldn't come in for my shift. It was a mandatory day off.

I smiled and thought about going back up to talk to Miss Emily, but I didn't think I'd be able to pull together enough guts to do it again. Instead, I went off to my bedroom and, after removing my shoes, crawled under the covers. Sleep, however, refused to come near me. I lay there for nearly an hour, trying everything from the obligatory sheep counting to the more exotic hermit crab surfing in order to make myself fall asleep, but nothing worked. Finally I just got up and went into the other room.

I flipped on the television and cycled through the channels. There was a news program (the adventure from the night before was the top story), but I switched it quickly. The last thing I wanted right now was to think about what had happened. I found a nice cartoon and sat watching it, although I couldn't seem to concentrate. There was a mouse, and a cat, and some big rocks, but I don't remember any of the actual plot. Of course, who ever remembers the stories from those things? Such unrealistic crap....

The program ended and another came on. My eyes started to wander, and I found myself looking at the pictures arranged around the apartment. I had a lot, some of my family, some of friends, some of Dumpty and his family. Dumpty and I really were close. My brother had been killed some years back, and Dumpty was about as close as I had ever come to having another one.

His family had welcomed me in, and I became like an uncle to his children. I had their pictures too, I thought, and I pulled out my wallet and looked through the random receipts and photos until coming to those of the Dumpty kids. Here was Kyle, holding the mitt he was so proud of. His father had taken him to a baseball game once, and he had brought the glove with him. Sammy Squirrel was his favorite player, and he had cheered for him nearly endlessly. When Sammy came up to bat for the first time, he fouled the first pitch off and Kyle had caught it.

It was the proudest moment of his life. He was on the Jumbotron and everything. After the game, he had gone down and had Sammy sign both the ball and his mitt. The ball was in a case on the mantle over the fireplace, but Kyle just couldn't bear to put his glove away like that. He used it all the time, but was very careful to preserve the signature.

I smiled remembering the time he had come running up and told me how he had gotten to play baseball in the park, and all the kids were jealous of his glove. I had to swallow to keep from sprouting a tear, and I moved on to the next picture. This was of Rachel, the middle child. She was a wonderful little girl who liked nothing better than dancing with her ballet class, unless it was riding horses.

She had always wanted a horse, but her father couldn't afford it. He kept telling her that maybe someday it would happen, but even as a young girl she knew it wouldn't. It was okay, though. Her father had paid for her to take riding lessons at the nearest barn, and I could remember going to her first competition. She had ridden like a champion, and it didn't matter that she didn't win first place. Her father had hugged her and taken everyone out for ice cream. She had been the happiest person I think I've ever met.

I moved to the last picture, of the eldest of the Dumpty clan. This was Michael, the jock of the family. He played every sport he could at the local high school, and was, in fact, one of the best athletes the school had ever produced. Of course, he wasn't just good at sports. Oh no, he was also incredibly smart. He had won tons of ribbons and plaques from various academic competitions, and was in the running for a national merit scholarship. Not that that would matter, since he was already getting offers from colleges, despite the fact that he was only in eleventh grade.

I sighed. These people were the closest thing I had to a family. My parents lived all the way across the Kingdom, and I very rarely saw them. My only brother, Mortimer, had died in a boating 'accident' some ten years ago. I had various aunts and uncles, but we didn't really stay in contact that much. They basically called whenever they read something about me.

I felt terrible. I couldn't imagine all the grief and pain that the Dumptys must have been going through. I put my pictures away and got up to go get some more orange juice. Passing by the front door, I noticed an envelope lying on the ground. I jerked open the door and looked both ways in the hallway, but it was utterly deserted, so I pulled my head back inside and turned my attention to the envelope.

I picked it up and turned it over, noticing my name was on it, but that was all. I opened it, carefully, and unfolded the single sheet of paper that came out. "Dearest John," it read. "I heard about the dreadful business with your partner, and I just wanted to offer my condolences. I know it can't be easy to lose a friend." It was signed

"An Admirer", and there was no return address.

I put both the envelope and the note in the basket I kept on the bookshelf next to the door for letters, and went to the kitchen to get my juice. After quickly downing a glass, I poured another and walked back to the chair. There are always cartoons on somewhere in the wide world of television, and I flipped through until I found another one.

The next thing I remember is a knock. I sat up straight and looked around. The sun had set, and the only light in the room came from the television, which was now showing some stupid sitcom about people in an apartment in New York. I glanced at the clock, in the glow from the television, saw that it was nine, then jumped up and turned on the lamp next to the chair. After turning off the television, I went to the door and opened it to the smiling face of Miss Emily. I welcomed her in and shut the door behind her.

III. The Three Blind Mice

The next morning was nice, with the dawn breaking through the low lying fog that seems to settle over the town like syrup over pancakes and shining through the window in my bedroom, waking me up. I rolled out of bed and stumbled my way down the hall to the bathroom, where I used the facilities, and then headed for the kitchen to make some breakfast.

On the way over, though, the blinking of the message light caught my eye. I hit play and continued on, already envisioning some nice toast with butter and maybe a surprise omelet. A surprise omelet is when you just throw whatever you can find in and hope for the best. I've decided that the chocolate puff cereal omelets are the best, and I was already leaning over to check if I had any of that magical cereal when what I heard stopped me short.

The message was from the captain. "Hi Monroe. I don't know when you'll get this, but get down to the station as quick as you can, ok? We have a possible development in the Dumpty case." The machine beeped and told me when the message had been left. I turned my attention back to the task at hand and decided regretfully that a cereal bar might be better than eggs. Turns out I didn't have any chocolate puffs anyway.

* * *

I left the apartment building at quarter past seven and got in my car. It was a good twenty minutes to the station, and I amused myself on the way over by listening to the radio. All the music seemed to be evenly split between 'golden oldies', those wonderful tunes that always seem to make me think of dentures floating in a glass, and 'modern rock', the term loosely applied to anything that sounded even remotely like a cat being beaten to death.

The news was still largely taken up with what had happened, and the talk station was busy deciding whether it was better to answer the voices or try to get them taken care of. Sometimes I wonder about the people calling into those shows. Right as I was about to give up, I found a nice salsa station and listened to that. Carumba.

I got to the old brick building that served as the station and parked out front. The station had, at one point, been city hall, but that was back before they built the new building over on Jackson Drive, with all its skylights and metal. We basically inherited the old building and suited it up for our needs. The courtrooms had been transformed into cells and the numerous offices were almost all in use.

I nodded to Charlie as I walked in and headed immediately to the right. The captain had his office in the right hand corner of the front of the building, which offered him an excellent view of the street and the shops on the other side. I knocked and heard him tell me to come on in.

The first thing I noticed on entering was that one of the captain's lights was burnt out. It gave the office a dingy feel that seemed to make me feel more at home. The second thing I noticed was the three mice that were sitting in front of the captain's desk. I grabbed a chair off to the side and watched as the captain turned to a television set mounted in the corner of his office.

He pressed play and there was the video from the park, but not to the part where we could see Dumpty. This was video taken from a few hours previously, if the time stamp could be trusted, which I assumed it could since technology rarely seems to cheat, despite the insistence of video game lovers everywhere.

I watched as people came and went, and then saw the three mice come out and shamble along. A woman had entered the screen now and was walking briskly toward the bridge, glancing for only a split second at the mice and trying to hide her grimace of disgust.

The mice on the screen turned and headed over, slowly surrounding her and drawing closer, like a net around some sort of sea creature that gets captured in nets. Crabs, maybe. The big one said something, and I silently cursed myself for not thinking to get audio equipment set up as well. The woman on the screen reached into her purse and pulled out a few coins, which she handed to the mice, and then moved on, walking much faster now.

The big one followed her until she was almost under the bridge, and then grabbed her purse and sprinted away with it. The other mice ran off after him, leaving the screen, and the woman looked frantic, holding her hands to her head and screaming bloody murder. It was almost funny, actually, like seeing a movie before the 'talkies'. I almost expected a little placard with "Aaaaaigh!" written on it to show up. Maybe a sudden ominous chord from a piano. The captain stopped the tape and turned to the mice. "Well?"

They leaned in and muttered to each other, then sat back and began reaching out with their hands. The biggest of them spoke up. "We'd like to remind you that we're blind and cannot see what you just tried to show us." The captain looked at me and winked.

"Well, Roscoe, that's you up there, big as life. You seemed to take quite a liking to that poor woman's purse. I gotta say, I never really pegged you as that type, my man. Now, if you wanted your own purse so badly, why couldn't you just go to Macy's? Was it embarrassment? You feel a little awkward buying a purse for yourself?"

"I am not gay."

"Nobody ever said you were. There's a difference between cross-dressing and being gay, or so I'm told. I just have one question. Where do you keep your dress?"

"I am not gay!"

"Then why did you take her purse?"

"I wanted the money!" He blinked. "Uh, I mean… I don't know what you're talking about."

The captain nodded. "Nice try. I think we've got you pretty cold this time Roscoe." The big mouse looked like he was about to say something, and then stopped. He had apparently just noticed his companions, who had stopped pantomiming and were staring out the window, one with his tongue hanging out. I followed their gaze across the street and saw a woman in a bikini top holding a sign that said "Eat At Joe's" bending over to pick something up. Roscoe smacked the mouse nearest him on the back of the head and whispered something in his ear.

"I can see!" This from the mouse that had just been slapped.

"Me too!" The third.

Roscoe turned back to the captain. "Oh my lord, it's a miracle!"

"Hallelujah!" The second again. All three looked at the captain, hope etched into their faces so deeply I could nearly read it.

"How nice," said the captain. "Look John, we got us a genuine miracle!" He had adopted the voice I had learned to associate with mocking, a mix between an Irishman and a southern farmer. It really did sound funny. "Praise the lord!"

"Praise the lord!" This from the third. Roscoe reached over and slapped him. "Look." The captain was back to his own voice. "I'm tired of this crap. We've had a lot of complaints about you three. You do realize that there's laws against purse snatching in this town, right?"

The three mice looked at each other and the middle one spoke. "Listen, sir, with all due respect. We don't think that you know what we're going through. It isn't easy for three blind mice to get jobs in this town. Now that we have our sight back it should be easier, but…" The captain was frowning and the mouse trailed off. "It's even worse when you're deformed…" That's when I realized where I had seen these guys before.

Three years ago we had gotten a call about a domestic dispute. We arrived on the scene and found three mice with large bandages over their tail stumps, a farmer, and his wife. It took awhile, but we finally got the story out of them. It seems that the mice had been panhandling around the farmer's property, which he didn't particularly care for, and he asked them to leave. It was a simple enough request, but the mice didn't like being told what they could and could not do, so they had set about making plans to rob the farmer's house.

Everything had been going good (they had set it up so they were there when the farmer and his wife weren't, a fairly common practice in the burglary world) until the farmer unexpectedly came home early. His wife had been the first one through the door and, on seeing the three mice standing there with bags stuffed with their possessions and heirlooms (and a bra in Roscoe's bag, oddly enough), chased them with a carving knife. She caught them, one at a time, and chopped off their tails.

It had seemed a simple enough matter at the time, but the trial was a mess. The mice were brought up on charges of breaking and entering, but because of the wife's admittedly overzealous actions they all got off almost scot-free. The jury figured that since the mice had already lost their tails that there was no need to put them in jail. If the loss of a vital limb didn't teach them their lesson, then the odds were that jail wouldn't do much either.

And so the mice were sentenced to public service, and I hadn't seen them since. Until now. The one on the end backed up the one in the middle. "We tried to get good jobs! Honest! It's just that no one wants us." As if on cue they all frowned, trying hard to convey the image of wounded puppies but only succeeding in creating a somehow grotesque tableau. Either that or a perfect postcard snapshot. Wish you were here, or something like that.

"Oh," said the captain, once again the caring southern Irishman. "I feel your pain. Look," he pointed at his bone dry cheek, "can't you see my tears?" One of the mice looked, but was immediately corrected by Roscoe's hand, and all of them suddenly found something highly interesting on the ground. "Sheesh, guys. I mean seriously. Did you think you'd get away with it? You're all still on probation. This is not good for you."

The mice didn't say anything. They looked like bad little boys who'd been sent to the principal's office. Admittedly, they were pretty ugly little boys, but still. The captain looked at me and winked again. Before I could say anything, he turned back to the mice and addressed Roscoe. "Now, Roscoe, I hear you have some information that we might find useful."

I learned later that Roscoe had been very open mouthed in the holding pens, and had let it loose that they wouldn't hold him for very long because he could lead us to Humpty's killer. I didn't know that then, of course, so I was quite a bit more interested in what Roscoe had to say. The mouse apparently didn't realize how the captain knew about his information (it's been my experience that when someone has a big mouth, they tend to get used to it and not really realize that what they are saying is being heard), and he took a defensive position, perhaps sensing that he might be able to bargain.

"I don't know what you're talking about."

"See, I wish I believed that, Roscoe. The problem here is that I know you know something, and I want that information. It seems to me that right now you're in a position where you could go back and spend a large portion of your life in prison, or you could tell me what I want to know and this part of the video could conveniently disappear." As if to emphasize his point he flicked the screen off. Even though I knew the captain was bluffing, it was powerful stuff. Oscar worthy, or at least People's Choice. Roscoe thought it over.

"You mean that?"

"Hey, do I look like the kinda guy that would lie to you?" The captain did his best to look like a big innocent teddy bear. It was actually pretty convincing, especially since he had dressed as just that for Halloween. That was a fun time. Imagine a gruff, red-faced Irish guy known for being one of the hardest cops you could ever meet dressed in a fluffy brown suit trying to act cute. Better yet, picture Sylvester Stallone in a pink bunny suit and you'd get the basic idea.

"Hmm." Roscoe, seemingly won over by the captain's cherubic face, looked at his compatriots and sighed. "Ok. I'll tell you what I know on two conditions. The first is the tape thing. The second is that no one knows who told you. If anyone finds out that we told you this, then we'd probably end up in several different pieces, and that's just not cool." I had the urge to say something about their tails, but I thought that might be a tad inappropriate, so I clammed up. The captain was pretending to think over Roscoe's offer. It was pretty obvious to me that he had already made up his mind before even bringing it up.

"Alright. Whaddya got?" Roscoe sighed, and then sat back in his chair.

"Well, that night we were hanging out near the Birch Street side of the park." I knew the Birch Street side. It was generally the only street bordering the park that was well used at night. Also there was a Victoria's Secret on the corner. I'm not sure if that would have had anything to do with their being there (especially since I always seemed to get the feeling that Roscoe would be more interested in Victor's Secret, if you catch my drift), but you never know.

"We were going through our routine, stumbling around, flailing, trying to get some cash for our troubles." At this he glanced down at where his tail should have been and looked wistful. "It was just after the concert got out."

There was a concert hall across from the park on the Birch Street side, and that night Uncle Mike and the Irregulars had played to a sold out house. The concert started at eight, so the odds were that Roscoe meant around ten thirty. "We were standing there, being blind and bumping into people, and then I got this really bad feeling in the pit of my stomach. I tried to figure out why, and when I looked up to the doors I realized I already knew." He swallowed. "It was Jack Henry."

The name itself caused all those in the room to sit back a little further. If the devil had an earthly form, then Jack Henry would be it. He had, at various times and in various places, killed more people then I think I've ever met. Jack Henry was like the crown prince of all crime. It's hard to impress the utter horror that accompanied the saying of that simple name.

I remember one story in particular. Some local gang leader had hired Jack to take care of a rival crew, and within a week there was an explosion at the crack house they had been using. Conveniently enough, every one of the rival gang members had been in the building. No one ever asked why they all had apparently been bound hand and foot.

Jack had gone back to get paid, and the gang leader apparently refused, because he got his throat ripped out. He also had his house burnt down with everything in it, including his family. Jack was dangerous and Jack was smart, a very bad combination. Roscoe looked down at his feet. The captain looked at him and frowned. "Well?"

Roscoe looked at him. "Well what?"

"Is that it?"

"Isn't that enough?"

"Well, no." Roscoe jumped up and became indignant.

"You told me if I told you then we'd get off!"

"Yea, but I thought it was something important. I don't give a flying crap about Jack Henry." That was a lie, but I don't think it mattered. "You didn't see him do anything? Go into the park, feed the pigeons, take a stroll, kill someone?"

"Well, no. When I saw him I told the other two that we should probably get the heck outta there, and we left." The captain shook his head.

"Did you at least see which way he went?" Roscoe shook his head. "Fine." He pushed the button for his intercom and summoned someone to take the three back into lock up. They all looked quite unhappy, but no one spoke. Roscoe apparently caught sight of his reflection in the window, because he started making kissy faces and fluttering his eyelids.

The other two pretended they didn't see it, and the captain was struggling to keep from laughing. Roscoe was in his own little world, and none of us really wanted to know what he was while he was there. Finally, after what seemed like an eternity, someone knocked on the door and took the mice away.

"Well?" As the door shut, the captain looked at me.

"I think he was telling the truth."

"Yea, I know. I was afraid of that."

"So, there're no leads?" He shook his head slowly, as though it hurt him immensely to move his neck. I asked to see the part of the video we were interested in, and the captain fast-forwarded to it. I watched as my partner came racing onto the screen from the direction of the clearing and stopped. He looked around, and then looked like he was about to go again when he stopped and looked over the edge.

He was looking for Waddles, that much was clear. Then something happened behind him, but off the screen so we couldn't see what it was. He had jumped, though, and turned around. I again reflected on the stupidity of not having audio set up. Now he was talking to someone, and it looked like he was getting mad. Then, suddenly, there was a flash as something came into the picture from where whoever it was had been standing and hit Humpty. He staggered back and fell over the edge of the bridge. Right before he hit the ground, the captain stopped the tape.

"I don't think we need to watch that." The tape was frozen with Humpty's head less than a foot from the ground. The look on his face was rather surprised, a "say what" face if I've ever seen one. The contrast between that and what he wound up like less than a second later was a bit much for me and I turned my eyes from the screen to the captain.

"What was the flash?"

"We aren't sure yet. We've been trying to figure it out, but we haven't gotten a definite fix on it yet. The best we can guess at is a hand. Horner's looking into it." I nodded. The captain turned the television off and looked at me. "Do you think you can come back to work?" I nodded and he smiled. "Are you sure? I don't want you overextending yourself."

"I'm sure."

"Ok. Good. Just, take it easy, ok?"

"Captain, this is me. I always take it easy." Lies.

"I know." Also lies. It was like some sort of a dance where both of us knew the right steps and just didn't care. "I just don't want you flying off the handle."

"No need to worry."

"Alright." He motioned me out the door, and I, feeling somewhat bewildered, left the office.

IV. Little Jack Horner

I made my way over to Jack Horner's office. Every person I passed either looked down at their feet or averted their eyes while I passed. What is it about the death of someone close to you that makes people treat you like an outcast? It was almost as if they were afraid my sorrow would somehow transfer to them if they looked me in the eye. I pushed these thoughts out of my head as I drew close to Jack's door. Jack was young, barely out of the academy, but he had already shown that he knew what he was doing numerous times.

The most memorable would have to be the Jack and Jill case. One day a few months back we were called by some frantic youngster bawling about her daddy. We got to the scene to find Jack lying face down in a pool of his own blood, the back of his head caved in. Jill was standing nearby, weeping and gibbering. We tried to get some information from her, but she was in no shape to talk. The little girl who had called us was in the house, and she was able to help us with a little bit of what happened.

It seems Jack and Jill had gone up the hill to get some "water", and the next thing she knew her daddy was swimming in 'the red pool'. When we looked up on the hill we found that they had apparently been making some of that good ol' moonshine in an old bathtub.

We took Jill to a women's home so she could get some help. A few days later, when Jill had come to some of her senses, we went and questioned her. She admitted the moonshine, said it was all Jack's idea. She told us that that night they had gone up to stir the liquid and had decided to try a few samples. Those few samples turned into some large glasses, and before too long they were both drunk.

Jill said she couldn't remember too much of what happened, only

37

that Jack had gone out to get some air and had slipped. When she made it to the bottom of the hill (a process of several minutes since the alcohol had made her about as mobile as a spinning top), she found Jack's lifeless body and had just started crying.

There were, of course, no sober and uninvolved witnesses, and so I had no way of proving that she was lying, although I had a sneaking suspicion she was. In the first place, we never found a rock covered in blood, which is something you would tend to expect if someone died from bashing his head open on one.

Also, the timing seemed a little off. If Jill's story were true, then there were about three hours unaccounted for. For some reason I found it tough to believe that even someone as drunk as Jill claimed to have been could have cried for three hours without attracting attention.

Anyway, we were at a standstill until Horner proved, rather conclusively, that Jack was dead before he ever rolled down the hill. He basically focused on the bruises and cuts from Jack's roll and found that the wounds were inflicted after the body was dead.

When we asked Jill about it, she seemed to faze out for a bit and then tried to change her story by saying that she had just remembered he fell and hit his head while he was at the top of the hill, and in the course of her checking to see if he was alive she accidentally pushed him over the edge. When we asked her why there were no signs of anyone trying to check the body, she folded like a cheap piece of plastic.

Jack, who was no great looker in the first place, was apparently cheating on Jill with a little tramp from the city. How he could find two women when I couldn't find one was beyond me (maybe because I had this odd little moral problem with paying for things like that, whereas Jack apparently didn't). Jill found out when he moaned out the other woman's name in his sleep, and she had gotten him to go up the hill with her for the express purpose of having it out with him in privacy (Jack and Jill had quite a large household, what with five kids and both sets of in-laws living under the same roof).

He admitted it and rubbed it in her face, then dropped the bomb:

he was leaving Jill for the other woman. Well, Jill couldn't have that. As he turned to go, Jill ran up behind him and gave him a big push. She hadn't meant to kill him, maybe just break his arm or something. The rock was just a happy coincidence.

She cleaned the rock off, then went back up to the still and drank until she fell asleep. When she woke up and realized what she had done, she ran, sobbing, to his body and fell on her knees. That's where we had come in. Now, we would have been able to put her away for quite a while, but by that time Jill had gone completely crazy, spouting all sorts of random things about rainbows and gumdrops, so she was found not guilty by reason of insanity and sent to the Happy Acres Mental Hospital.

Horner had made his mark with that case, and his ability had just been proven again and again, so I felt pretty much at ease. If anyone could figure this out, it was Horner. I reached out and knocked on the door, entering when I heard his somewhat shrill voice say, "C'mon in." Jack Horner sat in the corner of his office, staring intently at a video monitor, which was currently showing a single frame of the Dumpty video. I walked over and watched over his shoulder.

"Look at this." He zoomed in on the lower right of the screen, where the thing had come on and pushed Humpty off. It was grainy, but quite obviously a gloved hand. He turned and looked at me. "I've checked every frame where the hand is in the picture, and there really isn't much to go on. As you can see," he turned and pointed at the screen, "the perp was white." He was pointing at the slight sliver of skin that showed between the end of the glove and the end of the frame. "Also, he has somewhat hairy forearms." He hit a few keys and the section was enlarged, and then clarified, giving us a pretty good up-close view of the myriad little black hairs. He sighed. "I wish there was more."

I patted him on the back. "That's ok, Jack. At least you got this." I backed up a bit and stopped, still staring at the screen. I could remember a time, about 10 years ago, when Jack was just a scared teenager.

Having just joined the force, they gave me all the crap jobs. The older officers snapped up anything that promised to be gory or sensational, and I was left with the runaways and minor offenders. Don't get me wrong, I didn't have a problem with that. It's amazing how cruel some of these "fairy tale" folks can be.

A call came in one day from a woman who said she had a kid at her house whose parents had gone missing. He wouldn't talk or eat, just sat in the corner with his thumb in his mouth, crying. I headed out and when I got there she told me everything she knew. Earlier that day she had looked out her window and seen the poor kid walking aimlessly along. She thought he looked familiar, so she had gone out and brought him into her house.

When she found out how shaken he was, she tried to call his parents, but they weren't there. She waited, but eventually called the police because something didn't feel right. I agreed, and took the kid by the hand back to his house. When we reached the walkway to his front door, he dug his feet in and refused to go any farther, so I was forced to go up myself.

I knocked on the door and peeked through the windows, all to no avail. "Look under the mat." I was startled and turned around to look at him. He had clammed up again. I shrugged and lifted the corner of the mat, took the key I found there, and opened the door to the house.

I could tell right away something wasn't right. The smell was unbearable. I quickly looked through the living room and the bedrooms, but there was nothing to see, or at least there wasn't until I reached the kitchen. There I found a woman slumped in a chair with an obvious gunshot wound in her left temple. The gun lay a few feet from her hand. What drew me, though, was the sink. Something terrible had obviously happened here because the sink was covered in blood. The drain had been plugged on one side and the bowl was half filled with the red sticky stuff. I swallowed and slowly backed out of the room.

I found myself in the living room again, and so I went directly for the door, pausing just once to notice a pie sitting on the floor in the corner. I got to the kid and, after radioing in for more men, led him back to the neighbor's house. We went over Jack's place with a fine-tooth comb and found a number of interesting things.

The woman in the chair was covered with bruises, and a quick check of her hospital record showed that she had been seen for numerous broken bones and contusions within the last few years. Everyone figured it was the father, but we couldn't find him. Well, that's not entirely true. We found part of him.

We figured out most of what had happened, but no one will ever know for sure. Jack had been gone for the night, he was sleeping over at a friend's house, and the father had come home drunk for the millionth time or so. The bruises on her body were fresh, so we figured he must have been beating her and she snapped, killing him and doing something to get rid the body, except for the eyes.

Those she apparently decided needed to be put in a pie, and after baking it she left it in the corner with a card addressed to Jack. She then went back into the kitchen and ended her own life. Jack handled it really well, considering. Apparently his mother hadn't been the nicest person in the world towards him either, and though it obviously pained him to know that they were both gone, he didn't seem to horribly torn up over it. Some relatives had come and taken him, and he had grown up with a fascination with police procedures, eventually getting a job at the very station he had been in ten or so years ago.

All this passed through my head in a matter of seconds, but Jack, noticing my reverie, turned and looked at me. "You ok, Cap?" I nodded, and was walking out when I realized something. Jack wore glasses. I turned back and looked at him staring into the computer. I saw it again. The glasses were reflecting the computer screen.

I looked at the screen myself, and saw that Humpty was, indeed, wearing his glasses. He had once said that he was nearly blind without them, but that every once in a while he liked to not wear them. He thought he looked more debonair. I tried to get him to go with contacts, but he refused. I pointed to the glasses on the screen.

"Do you think you might be able to get a reflection off these?" Jack thought for a second, and then zoomed in on the section I had indicated. He punched in some things on the keyboard, and the new screen filtered a little. He typed something else and it got still clearer. It was now obvious that there was something there, but it was difficult to make out.

Jack turned to me. "I can definitely get something off here for ya. I don't know how clear it'll be, but I can get something." I nodded and clapped him on the back. That was all I needed.

* * *

I walked away from Horner's office feeling a bit better. At least there was something. We would get the guy eventually, but right now I needed something to do with myself. I had decided when Roscoe mentioned Jack Henry that it was too much of a coincidence, and that I had to find him and find out what he knew, so my first stop was the holding pen to get Roscoe. I had him brought into one of the interrogation rooms and stood outside steeling myself for what I was about to do.

When I opened the door and headed in, Roscoe looked up with a sneer. "Don't think I'm tellin' you anything." In that second I decided I hated Roscoe.

I sat at the chair on the other side of the table and put a folder down. "Well, Roscoe, I don't know that I like that idea."

"So? Why should I give a rat's..." He seemed to think better of it. "So?"

"Roscoe, Roscoe, Roscoe..." I was shaking my head. "Roscoe, do you have a family?" At this he perked up a little.

"Maybe. Will that help me to get out of this?"

"No, but I was just wondering. Do you know what it's like to be so close to someone that you feel like they're family?" Roscoe had clammed up again. Apparently if it didn't have to do with him getting off then it wasn't worth talking about.

"I'm going to assume that you have. I figure that somewhere in that overblown front you've got at least some small amount of feeling." It wasn't working. Every word I said pushed him further away.

"Fine." I reached into the folder and pulled out the pictures of Humpty's shattered body. I pulled one from the group and slid it across the table. "Take a look at that."

Roscoe tried not to, but in the end curiosity won out. He looked, and then almost retched. "Yea. See, that's not even the worse one. In fact," I said, rifling through the other pictures, "that's the best of them all." I pushed another one across the table. "That's the worst." Roscoe turned his head away and wouldn't look. "Bad, eh?" I got up and walked over to his side of the table.

"Listen." I put my hands on the front of his jail suit. "Humpty was more than my best friend, he was like a brother to me. Now someone has gone and killed him." I took the picture I had placed down second and held it in front of Roscoe's face, but he had closed his eyes. "Look at the picture, Roscoe!" I shook him, but he still didn't look.

"Someone killed my partner. Someone shattered his body all over the ground by the GW Bridge. His insides were spread out all over the wall! It was like a friggin water balloon, only with Humpty parts inside. Now look... at... the... picture!" I shook him to emphasize each point, and each time I shook I lifted him a little more out of the seat he was in. Finally, I saw his eyes slit open and he looked at the picture.

This one was from next to the bridge. It had been used to calculate splatter angles and such, mainly as a way of finding out how fast he was going and where he landed. Whoever had been doing the calculations had drawn the lines in red, which helped to contrast them with the black white and also had the added bonus of making the picture even more gruesome.

Roscoe twitched in my hands and came even closer to retching. I let him go, and he fell into his seat. I leaned over and looked him square in the eyes. "Humpty had a family. He had a life, and now he doesn't. Someone killed him in one of the most horrible ways I've ever seen, and I am trying as hard as I can to find whoever did it. I think you know something I want to know, and I think you'd better tell me."

He wouldn't even look at me. When he spoke, his voice was a whisper. "I can't tell you anything."

"I think you're lying. I think you know exactly where Jack Henry is, and I want to know." Roscoe looked at me oddly, then smiled slightly.

"What'll you give me if I tell you?"

"I might not hurt you." I cracked my knuckles while saying that. I've learned over the course of my career that cracking knuckles seems to work miracles even with the toughest guys.

Roscoe swallowed. "Okay." He leaned forward. "He's in town because of a special job. I don't know exactly what it is, but I know it's big. He's been hiring goons left and right. As to where he is, I haven't got a clue, like I told you before."

"Did he hire you?" Roscoe looked away. "I said," I was in his face now, "did he hire you?" No answer. "Fine. Maybe I can put in a good word for you down at the prison. Make sure all those inmates know exactly how you like it." His eyes grew wide. "That's right. If you don't tell me what I want to know, then every inmate in the state pen will find out that to you dropping the soap isn't such a bad thing."

"You wouldn't."

"Don't test me here, Roscoe."

"Fine. Yea, he hired me."

"How?"

"He gave me some money, moron. How do you think?"

"I mean, how did he contact you? And don't call me a moron."

"He had some guy come up to me in the park. Offered me a bundle of cash to..." He trailed off.

"To what?"

"That frikker..."

"What?"

"That frikker set me up!" He slammed his hands on the table.

"What do you mean?"

"He gave me money to take our little blind show to the next level. I took that woman's purse because Jack Henry wanted me to."

"Oh?"

"Yea. He friggin set me up."

"You mean Jack killed Humpty?"

"How the heck should I know?"

"Well, then how did he set you up?"

"He wanted us to get caught. The video cameras."

"Wait, are you saying that was the first time you stole a purse?"

"Yea. We aren't hardened criminals, man. Henry's guy gave us cash to stay around the bridge and steal some purses. He also told us that if we did good here then we would maybe get some work doing other stuff."

"Other stuff? What kind of other stuff?"

"How would I know? Does it look like I'm really able to do other stuff right now?"

"Ok, fine. Where is he?"

"I don't know."

"Where is he?"

"I don't know."

"Where is..." I cut off. "This is pointless. There's only one way we're going to resolve this." I grabbed his ear and pulled it, hard.

"Ow! What the heck are you doing?"

"Where is he?" I was yelling.

"I don't know!" I pulled harder. "I don't know!" His voice was cracking, he sounded like he was on the edge of tears. I reached into my holster and pulled out my gun.

"You ever had an earring before, rat boy?"

"What?" I pulled his ear down to the table and pointed the gun at it.

"Where," I pulled the slide, "is," I cocked the gun, "he?"

"I don't know." He cringed. I let go of his ear.

"There. Was that so hard?"

"What?"

"You heard me." I stood up and went to the other side of the table. "I think we're done here."

He started rubbing his ear and turned his head away. I grabbed the pictures I had been showing Roscoe, slid them into my folder, and started for the door. Roscoe waited until I had almost gotten out, and then spoke.

"Of course, if you're looking for whoever killed that Dumpty guy, then you're on the wrong track." I turned and looked at him.

"Oh? Then who killed him?"

"Now, you know I can't tell you that. To tell you the truth, I'm kinda glad that Dumpty got scrambled." I started to leave. "You can't make an omelet without breaking a few eggs!" I slammed the door shut. I was relatively sure that he was lying. Jack Henry had to have something to do with Dumpty's murder. He had to. I refused to believe it was a coincidence. But still....

I decided the first thing I needed to do was find Jack Henry and find out what was going on with him. I went and dropped the pictures on my desk, grabbed my coat, and headed for my car. As I passed the captain's office, though, he called me in.

"Well?"

"Roscoe let me in on a few things. I had to use a few special techniques, but he squealed pretty quick."

"Hmmm. So where are you going now?"

"I'm gonna try and find Henry."

"Are you sure that's wise?"

"Whaddya mean?"

"Well, if he killed Dumpty, then the odds are he can take you out too." I hadn't thought of that.

"Yea, but at least I know what I'm getting into. Humpty didn't know what was coming."

The captain grimaced. "Ok, but just be careful." He sounded almost paternal. I looked around his office, realizing for the first time that I had never really paid attention to the surroundings. There were plaques and pictures on nearly every available space, and one whole wall was taken up with a bookcase. He had pictures on his desk, and a computer. It seemed less like a captain's office and more like a stockbroker's.

"I didn't know you played trumpet." I was looking at a picture on the bookshelf of the captain holding a trumpet above his head. He was wearing a band uniform.

"Yea." He was looking wistfully at the picture. "That was after we won the championships." He sighed. "I don't play very often anymore." His eyes had glazed slightly, a sure sign that he was remembering days gone by. I slowly backed out of the office and shut the door.

V. Little Miss Muffet

Goons. At first I was a little disheartened, what with this being a rather large city and all. There were literally dozens of places that someone who needed goons could head. In a very concentrated effort at finding Henry quickly, I decided against driving around aimlessly and instead went straight to my desk and sat down, sorting through it all.

I decided my best bet would probably be to make some calls, so I jerked the top drawer open and grabbed the phone book I kept there. I mainly used the book to look up pizza parlors, doughnut shops, and all night Chinese places, but sometimes it came in handy for other things.

I was at a loss for where to begin. You couldn't just look up 'goons' and find what you were looking for, or at least I didn't think so. The more I thought about it, though, the less sure I was. I mean, after all, there are a lot of weird things going on in this city. I decided to check there first, but just as I was opening the book to the yellow section the telephone rang.

I sat there, staring at it dumbly for a second, and then remembered to pick it up. "Hello?" Silence... But not quite. I could hear some heavy breathing on the other end. "Listen, man. I don't know who you wanted to reach, but this is the police, and we don't take kindly to prank calls."

"Shhh. They'll hear you." I sat up in my chair. I recognized the voice, and even though the odds of someone listening to one side of a phone call being able to hear the person on the other end were relatively low, I thought it best to respect his wishes. Harvey Bumstein was what we in the business like to call a "mole", although the one time I referred to him that way he flipped out. See, Harvey was a wolf.

A few years back the King instituted a three-strike rule, aimed at curbing repeat offenders, of which we have quite a few. Harvey was a two-strike loser who had turned to snitching as one of the few ways left to him in order to avoid jail. It really was a very funny situation.

See, Harvey is not what you would call a hardened criminal. In fact, he has to carry an inhaler with him everywhere he goes. That and the valium he pops to ward off depression would seem to make him more of a candidate for an ulcer or a life of celibacy than that of a criminal, but life is funny sometimes. The first time I met Harvey, he was cowering in the corner of a wooden shack. It seems he had stopped a girl on the side of the road and propositioned her, only to get shot down. He followed her, intent on getting some small amount of revenge, possibly by hurling eggs at her, but when he saw her go into the cabin, he got other ideas.

He waited for her to leave, and then snuck inside, locking the old woman who had been in the only bed in a closet and donning some of her clothes. He lay in the bed for hours until he heard the door creak open, and then tried to scare the crap out of the poor girl.

Unfortunately for him, and somewhat fortunately for her, the girl had been taking self-defense lessons. She was, in fact, a black belt in karate. Harvey has, in fact, had very bad luck. Anyway, the girl decided she wasn't too fond of being followed and harassed by an overzealous wolf, so she decided to teach him a lesson... several times... with various limbs... Eventually a neighbor called in a domestic and I stepped in.

Sometimes I think Harvey would be an excellent case study for some psychology student, because when I talked to him it was quite evident that the worst he could have done to her was say boo, and even that would have sent him into a little convulsion of nervousness.

Yes, Harvey was a walking bundle of nerves. Since he hadn't done anything permanent, and no one besides Harvey himself had gotten hurt, there was nothing we could do, but the whole thing still went down on his record.

That was strike one. Strike two for Harvey came down when he got fed up with his neighbor. He had been living down on Quicksilver Lane, in a ramshackle old place sandwiched between a corner convenience store whose sole claim to fame was a signed photo of a crappy comedian with bright red hair, and (to quote Harv) "that stinkin pig." The way Harvey told it, the pig waited until ten o'clock at night and then cranked hardcore metal music as loud as he could in a deliberate attempt to drive the honest and hardworking citizens of the neighborhood (Harvey and an elderly turtle named Bob) utterly insane.

So, one night he decided that the pig needed to be taught a lesson and went to try and talk to him. When the pig refused to answer the door, however, poor little Harv snapped. He started huffing and puffing, something he quickly remedied with his inhaler. This only got him madder, though, and he started hocking huge loogies at the house. He seemed to possess an endless supply of the sticky green stuff, because he managed to get a little on nearly all of the pig's big picture window before the pig, crazed with fright, sprinted away to his brother's house.

Harvey, not quite getting the hint that he needed to stop, followed the pig and proceeded, beyond all possible explanation, to hock spittle at the brother's place. Both pigs then ran for their other brother's house, where they barricaded themselves in. Harvey tried to get them to come out, and then spit until his mouth was too dry.

When that failed to achieve the desired effect, he tried drawing them out with clever comments ("Hey pig, I think your momma was a pig! Huh? Whaddya think of that?" Harvey was not the brightest crayon in the box), but that didn't work either. Finally he decided to just climb up on the roof and drop down the chimney, Santa style. He clambered up the trellis and made his way, slowly (so as not to fall and crack his head open like that idiot Jack), to the chimney, where he jumped in butt first only to find a merrily burning fire waiting for him.

I was the second person called in, right after the EMS folks. Harvey walked around in a giant diaper for weeks, and he couldn't sit down for nearly two months. He was lucky he didn't die. It did make for a funny mug shot, though. One of the guys wanted to bring in a giant rattle for him, but we decided that might be a little cruel. Well, unusual, anyway....

So, that was strike two. We had several other key things we could have nailed him on (begging and the like), so we decided to try and capitalize on Harvey. He wanted to get out of trouble, and we wanted information. See, Harvey worked in one of the roughest bars in town. Well, he panhandled out front.

In exchange for our letting him alone, he gathered basic intelligence and let us in on some of the big stuff before it came down. To date he hadn't given us anything huge (one marijuana bust and a horrifying story about poisoned doughnuts that turned out to be a hoax), but that was ok. I waited for Harvey to decide that it was safe to talk again.

"You still there?" His voice sounded muffled.

"Yea, I'm here. How may I help you, Harvey?" I tried to use my nicest dignified voice, but it was a little out of practice and came out squeaky. I swigged some coffee to oil it up, and then decided that since one good turn deserved another, I was entitled to a doughnut. Unfortunately, they were all the way across the room, and I was tethered to the desk by the phone cord. I started trying to think of a way to get my hands on one.

"Ok. I was just inside Muffet's, and I passed a guy who was talking rather loudly about insurrection, and how the King needs to be overthrown, and... You know, stuff like that." I wasn't sure how to react. On the one hand, that sounded bad, but on the other hand, I needed my doughnut.

"Is that it?"

"Well..." He seemed reluctant.

"Come on, man. You know I got your little friends in a vice. You don't want me to squeeze, do ya?" I had given up on the dignified act and was giving some serious thought to the benefits of raspberry filling.

He seemed to think about it, but not very long. I wasn't worried.

If he didn't want to tell me, then he wouldn't have called in the first place. "Jack Henry."

Forgetting the doughnut (and that yummy raspberry), I sat up a little straighter, as if somehow he could tell I was more interested by my posture. Well, more like as if somehow he could see my posture and then make that assumption, but you get the point. "Wait. Did you say Jack Henry?"

"Yea. That's who it was. I think he might have tipped a few back, or something, but it was definitely Henry. It sounded like he was trying to recruit some people for something big." Suddenly I was really interested.

"Wonderful, Harvey. Thanks." I hung up. Well, that solved that. I threw the book back into the drawer and, shutting it, went to find out if anyone wanted to go visit a bar.

* * *

Twenty minutes later I was headed down to Muffet's with Jack Swanson and Steve Martell. The guys were in a rather jubilant mood. I hadn't mentioned to them why it was that they were coming with me, and Jack was telling us all about how one time he had won twenty bucks off this guy by jumping over a candlestick. It wasn't even a big one, which is what he seemed to find so funny.

At that time of day you woulda expected the bar to be nearly deserted, or even closed. Instead, the dirt parking lot was playing host to a small convention of rust colored cars, almost like a hillbilly auto show. We got out of the car and headed in, proceeding directly to the bar.

In the corner sat a few guys with grizzled faces, and Harvey was sitting by himself near the end of the bar. Any chatter or noise that had been going on dropped off almost immediately when we came in, and it didn't pick up at all as time went on. I motioned to the bartender.

"I'm looking for Jack Henry." He looked at me as if I were speaking Martian. I leaned over and spoke slowly. "Jack Henry. I need to talk to him, and you need to tell me where he is." He didn't answer. I turned and headed over to the table with the drunk guys.

"Hey there, chief." The others laughed as if that was the cleverest thing they'd ever heard. I laughed along with them, but a bit more subdued. After all, what good does it do you to take yourself too seriously? I stopped suddenly.

"That's good. You should do stand-up." They looked puzzled. I must have used a word that was a bit big for them. "Hey, I'm just lookin' for Jack Henry." Swanson and Martell had stopped dead in their tracks when I first used his name, but now they had gone off near the back, looking around to see if they could spot him. They had realized how important this little excursion was, and while neither had actually drawn a gun, both had their hands inside their coats.

The men at the table just looked at their glasses. I cracked my neck (again with the intimidation) and was about to speak again when I heard a noise from upstairs. I turned and looked at the bartender and then the noise came again. It was a whimper of pain.

I glanced at Martell and Swanson, who had both heard the noise, and we advanced to the stairs. Martell started up first, reaching the top in a matter of seconds and going directly to the door on the other side of the landing. Swanson and I joined him, and then I knocked on the door.

"Hello in there. Is everything okay?" No answer, but another whimper. I cocked my head. Swanson and Martell seemed to understand. I backed up, pulling my gun and covering the door while Swanson laid his hand on the doorknob. I nodded and he threw the door open. I held the gun steady, quickly looking for the source of the whimpering. It didn't take long, since the room was small and sparsely furnished. There was a bed, a sink, a chair, and a window. The bed was messed up and Jack Henry stood in a corner holding one hand over Miss Muffet's mouth. The other he was using to keep a knife held tightly to her throat.

I trained my gun on Henry's head, but I realized very quickly that he had the upper hand. He snarled, "Go away."

"I can't, man, and you know that." He didn't seem to like that idea, and pressed the knife a little harder to her throat, drawing a trickle of blood that made its way down her neck to stain the top of her "Coed Naked Water Polo" shirt. I thought quickly. "What's the point, man? You can kill her, but then what? I'll just shoot you in the leg and then we'll haul you off to prison. As it is right now, there's pretty much no way you'll ever see the light of day from outside a prison again. If you wanna add another death sentence to that, then go ahead."

I don't think he quite expected that. He looked from me to Swanson and then to Martell. He slowly inched his way to the left, across the wall on the far side and toward the window and the sink. I kept my gun on him. "Stop moving." He didn't listen. "Stop moving, Jack." He just glared at me and kept inching his way over. Then he was in front of the window.

He stopped and at first I was relieved, but then I realized what was about to happen. I started to yell out "no", but even before the word could fully form he threw Miss Muffet at us and dove through the window behind him, out onto the fire escape that protruded from the back. Miss Muffet crashed into Swanson, who in turn fell in front of Martell, who had started to run for Henry and instead tripped over the two of them, leaving both of the officers and Miss Muffet in a jumbled heap near the door to the room.

All this I gleaned from the corner of my eye as I sprinted to the window and hopped out. Henry had jumped from the edge of the escape onto the roof of the building next door and was running as fast as he could toward the back, which stood over a thin walkway that fell off on the other side into the lake. I leaped over the edge and landed on the roof running. "Henry, stop!" I didn't think yelling would help, and, as luck would have it, I was right.

He didn't bother to look back, and when he reached the edge launched himself off into space without a moment's hesitation. I lost sight of him for a second, and then I too was at the edge. As I jumped I noticed that he had cleared the walkway, and I had just enough time to say a quick prayer before, in less than a second, I crashed into the water.

It was colder than, well, something that's really kinda cold. Maybe an Eskimo's nose, or would that be considered a bit to politically incorrect? Ooh, I know. Colder than a frozen light pole. Those things are dangerous. People get their tongues stuck all the time. Anyway, I floundered for a few seconds before I managed to make it back to the surface, where I spit water out of my mouth and wiped the water from my eyes.

He was gone. I listened for the sounds of swimming, but couldn't hear any, so I slowly made my way to the small dock off to the left and pulled myself out of the water, sopping wet. I crossed over to the walkway and headed for the front door of the bar, shaking my head at the missed opportunity, but sure that I'd get another chance.

* * *

Inside, Swanson and Martell had called an emergency crew to come and take Miss Muffet to the hospital. She claimed that Jack had wandered into her room by accident, while he was looking for the bathroom. I thought her story was flimsy at best, especially considering what she was (another of our fair city's prosperous and popular prostitutes), but I let it go.

She seemed a little shaken up, and who could blame her? I asked her if he had said anything to her while he was up there. She shook her head, which meant that almost as soon as the door had shut upstairs, the three of us had come traipsing through the door, prompting him to whip out his knife.

I pondered all that had happened in the last 48 hours as we waited for the crew to show up. So far I had a dead partner, a mouse who was a rat, a rat who was a wolf, a prostitute who almost got her throat slit, and a master criminal who had barely slipped through my fingers. On top of that, I realized, I had never gotten my doughnut. This week was getting more and more interesting with every passing moment.

VI. Jack And The Giant Beanstalk

The ambulance crew arrived and loaded Muffet in the back. I watched as the doors shut and the large white box took off, headed for Marine General, the nearest hospital. Hanging my head, I headed back in and sat at a booth near the back, occasionally looking out the window, but for the most part simply thinking things through. I'm not one to see patterns.

When they showed me those inkblots in the academy entrance exam, all I could see was ink. The first time I told the guy that, he laughed and said I just needed to look deeper. I tried hard, but all I could tell him I saw was an idiot spilling ink all over some pieces of paper. Come to think of it, they've never asked me to retake that particular exam.

Anyway, I mention this because this time I sensed something was connected. The timing was just too perfect... I was turning everything I knew (about this particular case... I sorta figured that unrelated ideas, like my favorite food, wouldn't be too important) over in my head, looking for patterns and failing miserably, when Martell came over and sat next to me.

"Hey, don't take it too hard." He thought I was upset about losing Henry. "Everybody makes mistakes. I mean, look at me." I did. Martell was one of those cops who had taken it upon himself to personally ensure the prosperity of the city's doughnut shops. He had a waist like an inflatable beach ball: it just kept getting bigger. "Just last week I was chasing this guy and he got away." Swanson appeared next to him.

"Yea, a guy who was carrying a twenty-five inch television. That was a good bit of police work there, pal." He was laughing, and Martell joined him for a few seconds, then started hacking and gasping for breath.

"The point is," he continued after settling down, "it's not something to get upset about." He clapped an arm down over my shoulder, a large meaty paw that would have seemed at home on Smoky The Bear if Smoky were human and gained a few pounds. I glanced at him, then shrugged his arm off.

"I don't care about Henry. Something just doesn't feel right." He cocked his head.

"Ahh. Maybe you ought to get some dry clothes. I know if I was sittin around in wet skivvies then I'd be feelin kinda off too…" He looked down at his pants and I grimaced.

"Please don't ever do that again."

"What, say skivvies?"

"No, look at your crotch."

"Oh. Sorry there, Cap. I forgot. On the job and all." He grabbed a half filled mug of beer from off the table and swigged it down. "We have to act a certain way when we're on duty. I gotcha." He winked, or tried to. Instead his cheek jiggled and his eye squinted. I shook my head and closed my eyes.

When I opened them again, the first thing I saw was the clock. If time flies when you're having fun, then it really flies when you've just screwed up something big. Or when you throw your clock gets thrown out the window. Of course, that might just be me. I've never been quite like everybody else. Maybe I was dropped on my head as a kid, or something. Actually, it was probably several times….

"Ok, folks." I addressed this to Martell and Swanson. "We gotta get back." I stood and headed for the door, pulling my keys from my pocket as I went. The car was near the door, and it didn't take me long to reach the car and unlock the door. After sliding in behind the wheel, I unlocked the doors for the other two.

We left the lot and made the left to head back towards the station. I was about three minutes out when I noticed two people huddled on the street corner, one glancing around suspiciously while the other nonchalantly kept both hands in his pockets and looked at the ground. I drove past, then slowed down and turned at the next street, parking at the curb and switching the engine off.

I turned and told the other two what was going down. "The guy with the coat back there, that's Ricardo 'Jack' Montoya." Martell nodded. "The other guy I've never seen, but the odds are it's some sort of drug thing. I'm goin' out. Martell, you go up to the next block and head down from that way. Swanson, you do the same thing, but from that way." I realized I had crossed my arms over my chest while pointing and quickly fixed the problem. They both nodded, and we left the car.

Putting my hands in my pockets, I ambled my way down to the corner, turning to head back the way we had just come. I could see Ricardo at the corner, his friend moving off up the street, toward where I hoped Martell would soon be. When I reached the curb Ricardo noticed me and started to walk the opposite way from his friend, toward Swanson. I crossed and jogged up to Ricardo, hailing him when I was about three feet behind. "Hey Ricky! How's it goin', man?"

He stopped and turned slowly. "Oh, hey Cap. It's goin great. How's it goin with you?" I smiled. This was gonna be easy.

"Oh, it's goin great. I just thought I'd come over and, well, see what you've been up to. You know me, always concerned with the well being of my friends." The look on his face told me I was no friend of his. "You know, make sure everything is kosher. Don't want you ruining your parole." Ricardo was on parole for possession. We couldn't prove intent to sell, but we were relatively sure we would nail him eventually. It was his first strike and there was a general consensus that we'd see him again.

Ricardo looked nervous, but when he spoke he had adopted a 'tough guy' voice. "Oh, man. Of course I'm bein' good. All that drug crap? Yea, I don't even touch that stuff anymore." At the same time he put his right hand in his coat pocket, which made me believe that he was touching the stuff, both physically and metaphorically. The hands always give you away.

"Hmm. See, I really wish I could believe that." I could see over Ricardo's shoulder that Martell was on his way up. I only hoped that

Swanson was behind me somewhere. "But," I continued, "I was just drivin by up here," I motioned with my hand, "and I coulda sworn I was seein' an honest to god drug deal. Now, please tell me I'm mistaken, 'cause I sincerely hope that I'm wrong."

He blinked, then swallowed, trying to decide what to do. "Well?" I asked the question as if I expected an answer. These street punks are all the same.

"You're mistaken?"

"Oh, come on man. Say it with conviction."

"Y-you're mistaken! You don't know what the heck you're talking about!" His nervousness had won out, and he abandoned the tough guy voice.

"That's better. Course," I moved closer, "I don't like bein' told I'm wrong." He looked in my eyes and something must have snapped, because Ricardo turned and sprinted off. I watched as Martell, who had seen the whole thing, stuck his arm out and clotheslined Ricardo, throwing him down on the pavement.

If I had to isolate any one thing that I love fat guys for, their ability for the clotheslining would have to be pretty high up there. Also the dancing. I love to watch fat guys dance. Martell was yelling at Ricardo immediately, screaming that he needed to turn himself over and put his arms above his head. I started to head toward Martell, intending to help him out, when it happened.

I've been told that in situations of extreme duress it's relatively common to think time is slowing down, almost as if everything has suddenly gone into slow-mo. Well, that's a real fairy tale. I mean, this was about as extreme of a situation as you can get, but it flew by, and most of my recollections are kinda blurry.

Martell was yelling at Ricardo, who had started to turn, and he was reaching into his back pocket to grab a pair of cuffs when his body suddenly lurched forward, as if a linebacker had rammed him from behind (clipping, I think it's called). He looked up, and then fell forward, over Ricardo's body, and as he fell I saw a mist of blood coming up from where he had been. I watched in horror as his body flopped onto the ground, looking oddly like a dead fish (of the whale species, unfortunately). The sound must have been lost in the hustle and bustle of everyday life, because I never heard it.

The very first thought that went through my head was that I ought to help. The second was that if there was someone down there shooting, then I would probably be the next shot, and I should try and get out of the way. At that, I threw myself to the side, aiming for a small doorway that turned out to be the entrance to Sing Sung's Chinese Delicacy Market. I rolled into a large display of fortune cookies, knocking the whole thing over and covering myself in crinkly plastic wrapped packages.

I had made the right decision, though, because even as I was leaving the ground I felt something go whizzing by my cheek. Pulling my gun, I jumped out of the pile and headed for the door as Sing Sung started yelling at me. "What you doing? You come back here, pay for this!"

I poked my head out, scanning the street for something out of the ordinary. Apparently other people had heard the shots, because the streets, which hadn't been overly crowded in the first place, were now utterly deserted, giving the whole scene a showdown feeling. The only thing missing was a tumbleweed (or maybe a newspaper, which seems to be the modern day equivalent) and the far off strains of a piano tinkling Ragtime or some other early western hit. I couldn't see anything, but that didn't mean much. The shooter could very easily be sitting in a window somewhere beyond my line of sight.

I pulled my head back in, noting several things at once. Ricardo had disappeared, apparently pulling himself out from under Martell's body (not really sure how he managed that). I wasn't too worried, though, because he was tracking Martell's blood with every step. There was the sound of sirens in the distance, meaning someone had already alerted the rest of the force, and Swanson had yet to turn up.

I turned to find Sing Sung pining away as if his cookie display were some family heirloom, and then sighed and hung my head, noticing for the first time that the remnants of a fortune cookie were plastered to the front of my coat. I had really done a number on that poor display. There was a slip of paper lying on the ground, one of the fortunes, and I reached down and grabbed it. 'Today will bring you good fortune and long life.' What a crock. I always knew those stupid things were full of crap.

* * *

A large contingent of the Breco force arrived within ten minutes. When most crimes are committed, you'd be lucky to get four cops. When the crime involves the death of another cop, though, everyone wants in on it, and they typically will drop what they're doing and head to the scene. This was the sort of emergency that the donut folks dreaded, 'cause it really cut into their profits. I waited until I saw the captain weaving his way through the gathering throngs, all of whom seemed bent on catching a glimpse of some blood. I almost pitied them. What is people's fascination with violence?

He was heading past the doorway when I reached my hand out and grabbed his shoulder. "Holy…" He turned, jumpy as a cat.

"Hey, it's just me."

His demeanor softened dramatically. "Oh… John. You scared the crap outta me."

"Sorry."

"Seriously. I'm an old man. You just can't do that." For the first time I realized the truth behind those words. The captain had been around seemingly forever. Well, at the very least, he had been around the entire time I had. I wish I could say he was like a father to me, but that would be a lie. I can understand the need of some people to have a mentor, or a father figure, in their occupation, but it always seemed kinda pointless to me. Now, though, as I saw how old he looked, I felt sad. As bad as this was for me, it had to be even worse on him.

"Sorry."

"It's ok. I'll live." He glanced at the spot where Martell had fallen, and then turned back to me. "I mean, I'll be fine." I agreed. Death was not something I wanted to talk about right then. "So, what happened here, John?"

That was the captain I knew, large and in charge. "Well, we were heading back to the precinct when I spotted Ricky Montoya in what looked to be a compromising position, and I decided that it was in the best interests of the city if I made sure everything was okay." I related the story to him, ending with the gunshots and leaving out the bit about the fortune cookies. A guy's gotta have some secrets.

The captain listened and nodded as I went along. It wasn't the most thrilling tale, but such is life. If I was meant to tell stories I woulda been a politician. At the end, I asked if Swanson had shown up yet. At this, the captain bit his lower lip. "Oh no…."

"John…."

"No…."

"John, we found him a block up. Someone really laid into him. There was a tire iron laying on the ground next to him. Won't know for sure 'til the coroner's done with him, but we're assuming he was attacked from behind, and it just kinda went from there."

"So it was fast?"

"We're hoping so."

"What else happened to him?"

"Well…" He trailed off. "Are you sure you wanna hear this?"

"I have to."

"Several key parts of his body were, well, not a part of his body anymore."

"Key parts?"

"His feet, his hands… his head…."

"His head?"

"Yea… They put his head on his feet."

"And his hands?"

"In his mouth." I felt myself swaying. I wanted to puke, to scream, to kick something… I wanted to express my rage. For a few seconds I could almost see how some people can commit murder. I felt the anger… I shook my head. Three dead cops in less than three days. That has to be some kinda record.

* * *

62

The next few hours were a blur. The medics wanted me to go to the hospital, but I refused. I had just been up there, and there was absolutely nothing wrong with me. I told them what they really needed was some sort of a fortune cookie medic, but they just looked at me like I was nuts, and then went back to trying to reason with me.

I eventually told them I wasn't going, and that was that, and they didn't seem convinced, but they had no choice. I needed to get somewhere and think. A cop killing is not a common thing, and three is way out there, so I couldn't help seeing all of them as being connected.

I made my way slowly back to the station, stopping every once in a while in an attempt to get some fresh air (and to fight the uncontrollable urge to let my breakfast re-enter society). I eventually got where I was headed, and pulled my car into the lot. It took me several minutes to actually get out of the car, though. I was overwhelmed with feelings.

I mean, less than two hours before there were two living, breathing (as if there are any other kind) human beings sitting in the backseat of my car. One of them was fat, granted, but they could easily have been destined for great things. I mean, for all I knew, Martell could have become the next president.

I spent a few seconds thinking of that and then quickly dismissed it as wishful thinking. The only thing Martell could have been president of was his own fan club. On the other hand, you never know. The fact that they were no longer alive, no longer a part of society, that was terrible. I couldn't bring myself to leave the car. Why should they be dead while I was still around to threaten the world with excessive amounts of regurgitated cereal bar? By that time, I was fighting back tears. The stress was just a little overwhelming, you know?

The thought that finally got me moving was a very morbid one. If they could die, then so could I. When that one entered my mind, I snapped forward in my seat and then looked around, suddenly paranoid. I couldn't see anyone except for the Chicken man up the street (a man paid to stand around outside the Chicken Shack encouraging people to pick their favorite part ahead of time... they had even painted a little grid on him with the name of each part written in blood red paint). I didn't really think the Chicken man would try to kill me (I have, on occasion, joined him for coffee and doughnuts after work... he's an ok guy under all those feathers), but I suddenly knew that didn't mean squat. Nothing was as it seemed anymore. I grabbed the handle and swung the door open, stepping out onto the blacktop and taking a deep breath.

Death was on my mind, and it wasn't very pleasant. I shut the door and locked it (I continually find it amazing that our society is in such a state that even a cop's car, in front of the friggin police station, is not safe from thieves), then headed into the station, where I strode confidently down the hall (stopping just once to grab a raspberry doughnut since, death or no death, my stomach was hurling garbled obscenities at me) and flopped into my chair.

My head was reeling, so I placed the doughnut on the desk and put my face in my hands. Death. The sound of the word was terrible, the thought even worse. Everything seemed contaminated with it. Everything I saw looked bloody, everything I heard terrifying. Heck, even the smell was one of death. Death and raspberries.

That was definitely not a thought I wanted. I tried to push my mind somewhere else by thinking of the Bahamas, of Antarctica, and even of a Sports Digest swimsuit shoot. When all of those little fantasies (my favorite was the one with the swimsuits, for some odd reason) ended in a pool of blood, I decided to do some paperwork. There's nothing like drowning your sorrows in the mindless tedium of putting graphite to dead trees.

I reached for the first item in my little in and out box, trying not to remember that Dumpty had given me the box last Christmas after telling me repeatedly I needed to organize. I glanced at the piece of paper and started to crumple it up. Just some stupid memo about the annual visit.

See, the King thought it was of the utmost importance to try and visit every one of his lands at least once a year. The theory was that if he showed up in person, then the people would love him and not try to forcibly enter his castle with large guns. I thought it was kinda pointless, but I'm just a lowly detective, so what do I know?

I made a little ball out of the memo and was about to shoot it for two (a very easy task since the trash bin was less than three feet from where I sat, but you gotta take your victories where you can find 'em) when I suddenly thought of something. Harvey had said that Jack was talking about insurrection and taking down the King. He was looking for goons for something big. My heart started beating hard. I uncrumpled the paper and took a closer look.

He was coming in three days, and we were supposed to volunteer for guard detail. The King had his own personal guards, but the routes he was going to take would need to be staked out and everyone seemed to feel that we should be on hand in case something happened. The memo was signed by Mike Rizzoli, head of security and the King's second cousin. Well, that could easily explain the Jack Henry situation. But what about the dead cops?

I sat there, slowly scratching my chin and puzzling through it. If, for the sake of argument, Henry were planning some sort of attack on the King, then why would he want to kill cops? Or was I barking up the wrong tree, trying to make a connection where there wasn't one? My head started hurting, but I think that had more to do with the fact that I hadn't had any water all day than with the fact that I was thinking too hard, although I guess you can never be too sure.

I got up and headed to the fountain. Just as I bent over I heard someone walking around behind me, and I turned to see who it was. Unfortunately, I didn't stop moving forward, and I splashed water all over the side of my head. I stood up, water dripping from my hair onto the front of my shirt, and glared at the young officer who had diverted my attention. He was laughing. "Something funny there, crank?"

"Crank? What the heck does that mean?" I've never been too good with the being clever, so instead of answering I just lunged at him. He backed up, then laughed nervously. "Sorry man. My bad." He backed off some more. "My bad." Then he turned and walked off, muttering something under his breath.

Glaring after him, I turned back to get my drink, and then I had it. If Jack Henry were trying to set up some sort of attack on the King, then he would need to divert the attention of the local authorities. If they were looking elsewhere, then he would have a much easier time. What better way to divert a cop's attention than to kill another of his ilk?

Suddenly pieces started falling into place, sort of. Sometimes the truth is like on of those pictures with the old lady and the young lady. You just have to look at it the right way, and you can see what you want.

This was like that. I headed down to the captain's office, meaning to let him on my suspicions, but realized he would still be out at the scene. That stopped me faster than a bird flying into a window, and I headed back to my desk. I decided that if I was right, then I should see what else we might have that could fit in.

My phone started ringing as I drew near, and I jogged the last few yards, grabbing the phone and letting out a quick "Speak to me."

"Hi there." The voice was low and measured, very malevolent sounding. Reminded me oddly of a crocodile, which is odd since I have yet to meet a talking crocodile (or, for that matter, a normal crocodile). "Am I speaking to Detective Monroe?"

"Yea…" I was cautious. "Who is this?"

"Oh, come now. You mean to tell me you don't know?"

Suddenly I realized I did know. I thought about lying, but it would be no use. He would know. "Hi Jack. How're you?"

"Oh, I'm good. I think the question is how are you? You've had a rough couple of days."

"Cram it. It's your fault, so don't give me any of this sorry crap."

"Oh, but John. I'm just trying to share my sympathies."

"I appreciate it. Really." I was trying to hold back on the sarcasm, but it was dripping out the edges like grease from a pizza.

"Well. Testy, aren't we? I was just going to tell you that if you want Ricky, you can have him. I tried to tell him that he should have been more careful, but he just didn't listen."

I perked up. "Where is he?"

"Ninth and Wesson. If I were you I'd hurry. By my watch you have about..." he trailed off, "ten minutes." He hung up. I glanced at my watch and saw that in ten minutes it would be four twenty. That seemed oddly appropriate. Four twenty was the police code for marijuana, something that was referred to as "magic beans" in the city.

Some bright individual had decided that Jack's adventure in the clouds was the byproduct of a drug related high, and since it had to do with a large plant, then it musta been pot. We had a hunch that Ricky was a major dealer, and that's how he got the nickname Jack, at least around the station. Horner wasn't to keen on it, but I've never been to fond of people calling the can the john, so I wasn't overly sympathetic. I grabbed my keys and rushed out the door, leaving my coat flung over the seat.

* * *

Ninth and Wesson was about ten minutes away from the station, but that's if you were driving the speed limit and obeying most of the traffic laws. In my desperation to reach Ricky before whatever was going to happen happened, however, I developed a new sense of awareness, one that said traffic laws were for the weak, and managed to make it to the spot in just under five minutes.

Ninth and Wesson was the location of an abandoned building that had once housed a Giant's Bane Supermarket. The windows were boarded over now, and the grass out front had turned brown from neglect. We had been here many times in the past on drug calls. People were constantly accidentally making their way inside and, accidentally of course, falling on needles and choking on bongs that magically appeared in their mouths.

I pulled my gun and ran to the front door, kicking it in and rushing inside. The place was as dark as pitch, but I could just make out the outline of a human figure about twenty yards from me. I sprinted over and used the little flashlight I have on my keychain to see what

I had. It was Ricky, that much was clear. His mouth was gagged, and he was bound tightly to a small wooden chair. I pulled the gag off first.

"Help me!" he was screaming. I moved around behind him, looking at the knots that were binding him. "Come on, man. It's not like you've got all day."

"Hey, Ricky?" I was pulling at the first of the knots. There were three.

"What?"

"Would you mind shutting up? I've got a headache." He didn't seem to care.

"You think I care? There's a bomb about to go off, and you're not getting me out of here!" His voice rose several octaves as he let the last bit out. I tried not to listen. Bombs scare me.

I finished with the second knot and moved on to the third, stopping only to glance at my watch, noting with alarm that I had just under a minute left. Ricky was going nuts, screaming and, by the smell, peeing in his pants. He was really scared. I got the last one loose and gave him a shove.

"Run!" We both sprinted for the door. He reached it first and ran through. I followed him, and we reached the other side of the street just as the bomb detonated. The other side of the street featured an old, run down apartment building with a waist high brick wall enclosing a small grassy yard. Ricky was slightly in front of me and had already vaulted over the wall. I had my hand on the wall and had just jumped up as the concussion hit.

I felt my legs being lifted up higher than I thought they could go, and then I was flying backwards. I fell down in an arc, landing on my back on the other side of the wall, where I could see a plume of smoke rising as debris fell haphazardly out of the sky. I thought I saw a fluttering piece of paper falling toward me, and only had about a second to move my head when I realized it was a very sharp piece of metal sign that could quite easily have cut something vital off my person. Rolling over, I spotted Ricky struggling to his feet, looking like he was gonna run again.

I grabbed the gun from my holster and pointed it at him. "Freeze." He listened quite well, stopping in mid step with his arms bent away from his body in twin "L" shapes and looking back at me. I slowly staggered to my feet. It hurt to breathe, and I suspected I had at least one broken rib. It was really weird. In my entire career, I had never seen so much action. I was beginning to feel like some sort of superhero. All I needed now was some sort of a catch phrase. Maybe "Banzai!" or "Bite me, street scum." Actually, sometimes the basics are better. Maybe I should just use "freeze."

* * *

This time when the medics tried to get me to the hospital, I relented. It's odd, but when you feel like someone is smashing you with a sledgehammer every time you try to breathe, you tend to listen to medical personnel. Before I would let them take me, however, I made sure someone slapped some cuffs on Ricky. If Ricky was working for Jack, then he had to know something.

I saw the captain coming over, and I tried weakly to motion him over. "Lookin' good there, John."

"Thanks. Your honesty is refreshing."

"Hey, that's me. Refreshing to the core." He smiled, but it looked fake.

"I'll be fine, Captain." He nodded, but still looked unconvinced. "Look, just make sure you get Ricky in, ok? He called me."

"Ricky?"

"Jack Henry. He called me and told me to come here and save Ricky. There has to be a reason, and I'd be willing to bet that Ricky knows it."

"Ok, John. I'll take care of it. You just get better, ok?" He left and talked to one of the officers, who headed over to where Ricky was sitting, being treated by a medic. The officer stood by and waited until the medic nodded at him, and then he slapped the cuffs on. Once Montoya was safely in the back of a cruiser, I let the medics lift me into an ambulance and we raced off into the setting sun. It was kinda hard to believe that it was only yesterday that Dumpty had died. I can remember wondering idly if the hospital had a frequent visitor program, and then blackness settled over me.

VII. Goldilocks and The Three Bears

My eyes opened slowly, adjusting to the light that was streaming through the open windows. Everything was blurry for a moment, but shapes quickly distinguished themselves and I became aware of someone softly breathing very close to my left shoulder. I turned my head slowly and encountered a large mass of curly brown hair. Someone had apparently taken it upon themselves to stay with me. Either that or there was one hairy dog lying next to my head.

I looked around the rest of the room, deciding that if the unknown visitor were anything like me then waking him (or her) up would only result in some crabby comment (generally something involving words I was always told I shouldn't say, like "son of a purple headed monkey butt"). Remarkably little had changed since the last time I had looked around a hospital room, but since that was only a day or two ago it wasn't much of a shock. I noticed that there was an IV drip in my arm again, and breathing was somewhat difficult.

The doorknob slowly turned and the large wooden door creaked open, revealing a nurse wearing the apparently regulation white dress and carrying a clipboard. She frowned when she saw that I was up but my visitor was not, and then tiptoed over to my right side.

"Good morning, sleepy head." Her voice, even in its current lowered state, was perky and upbeat, precisely the kind I normally detested. Now, however, I couldn't help but smile. It takes too much energy to detest things. This is why old folks will gripe about things but very rarely join street gangs.

"Mornin' beautiful." I tried to make my voice drawl but failed miserably. I absolutely suck at foreign accents, and for me southern is about as foreign as it gets. She giggled somewhat self consciously, and looked at the chart.

71

"Well, it looks like you're ok, for the most part. You were lucky." Her finger was pointing at me and wagging up and down in a gesture I had always associated with bad dogs and four letter words that rhyme with "poop". Oh, wait. That is the word.

"Only a rib. By all rights you should be dead." Her voice lowered several decibels over the word dead, as though she were a tad squeamish when it came to death (something I found a little ironic), but went right back to normal as she continued. "Or at least in a full body cast." She smiled again, a broad bit of white that reminded me dully of the Cheshire cat, and I grimaced. I tried to remember what had happened to send me here, but had only a vague recollection of fire and falling things, and I knew that I had gone after Ricky, and that he was in an old supermarket....

"Did I hit my head?"

"Mmm?" She hadn't been paying attention, at least to my words. She was mesmerized by my scar. I have this scar on the left side of my neck. It's really gruesome looking, but the story behind it is really rather funny. See, I was chasing this guy one time in the dead of winter. He had stolen something like two hundred dollars worth of music from King Tut's Music Emporium ("Reeds? Yea, we got reeds...") and was now trying to get away.

I was after him, closing the gap slowly but steadily, when he suddenly sidestepped into a doorway. I tried to stop but found it a little difficult as the sidewalk was currently icier than a frozen something or other.

The basic point is that my upper body wanted to stop (the head was in favor of it, at least), but my lower body thought it wise to go with the inertia, and since the mobility of my body was being determined by the lower half, it won out. I slid right by the doorway, catching a glimpse of the thief smiling at me, and ran face first into a telephone pole. I fell down, dazed, and only came fully to when I felt the guy kick me in the ribs.

He started kicking me in other places (the arm, the legs, the "twins"), but it wasn't until he pulled back to go for the head that I jerked myself up. His kick got me in the shoulder, and I staggered to

FRACTURED

my feet while he reached in his pocket and drew out a switchblade.
"You shoulda just let me go, man." I coughed, spewing blood onto
the pavement and made some remark that I think was supposed to be
clever but actually came out sounding more like a random barrage
of unintelligible grunts. The guy apparently had no more luck in
understanding what I said than I did, because he shook his head and
then lunged at me with the knife.

I was able to spin to the side as the knife came by, so it only
sliced through a few of the layers of skin on the side of my neck
instead of going right through my throat. His lunge had carried him
forward, and as I spun I reached out and gave him a nice push, right
into the phone pole. He didn't like that much, I guess, because he too
fell over.

I kicked him a few times (just to let him know what it felt like),
then drew my gun (something I had forgotten I had, probably due to
the hitting my head) and aimed it at him. Eventually I ended up
getting something like twelve stitches, and the scar has remained a
useful tool for picking up women ever since. Actually, come to think
of it, that isn't really a very funny story....

Anyway, the nurse wasn't listening because she was admiring,
and so I had to ask her again about my head. "My head. Did I hit it?"

"Yes." She shook her head (Why do people shake their heads to
help clear them? Do they think that maybe the cloudiness will
suddenly fly out of their ears if only they shake hard enough?), and
then adjusted her uniform. "You want to know all of it?" I tried to
nod and found it to be just over my current pain threshold, but she
got the idea. "Alright. The worst of it is the rib. You also knocked
your head pretty hard, but not bad enough to create any lasting
damage. You've got some scrapes and a couple contusions, but that's
about it." There was a moan. "Oh, you've also got a visitor."

The furry head next to me had started to move. I looked down,
waiting until I could make the connection, and then beamed when
the head raised and I was looking in the face of Miss Emily. "Hi."
Her voice was sleepy.

"Hi. How'd you get in here?" The nurse quickly and quietly made her way out, leaving the door slightly ajar.

"Well…" She blushed, and I was instantly struck with how cute she looked. That, of course, was followed almost instantly by the fact that I had never, so far as I remembered, thought anything was cute, including those little monkeys with the diapers. I wondered if I had hit my head harder than they were telling me. "I had to tell them that you were my boyfriend."

Now, there are technically two things wrong with that. The first is that we weren't, to the best of my knowledge, that serious yet, so technically she was lying and could get herself in a lot of trouble. I, however, didn't care, and wasn't planning on telling anyone. The second problem was that I absolutely detest the word boyfriend. It sounded, I dunno, slightly juvenile.

"That's ok." I pulled one of my hands up and stroked her cheek. "I won't tell." She laughed.

"When I saw on the news what happened I hurried down here as fast as I could. Listen." She pulled away from my hand and stared me in the eyes. "I like you. I'm not going to lie, and screw all that hard to get stuff. I like you a lot. I was worried and I had to see you." She stopped, seeming to want something in return.

"Well, I like you a lot too." This really was juvenile. I felt like I was back in the third grade, chasing girls and being mean just to cover up for the fact that I liked them. I suddenly was overwhelmed by the sensation that I had somehow blacked out and woken up a good twenty or so years in the past. I became convinced that if I looked to the door I would see my mother, worried beyond belief, and for a fleeting instant was concerned about missing too much school, but then Miss Emily smiled, and I was suddenly waving goodbye to all my cares.

"Good." She slipped her hand into mine. "Now don't go getting yourself killed."

"Not if I can help it."

We talked for hours. I told her all about myself, starting with my earliest memory. I must have been about four years old, and I was trying to catch a robin that was poking its head in through the open window above my head. After trying to grab it and discovering that it was just out of reach (a tough concept to grab for a four-year-old), I went and found a little box, one of those things with the blocks inside and the shapes to push through.

I put the box down on the ground and stood on it, only to find I was still a bit off, so I toddled off and got another box, put it on top of the first, and climbed on top of the whole mess, only to fall right off on my butt when the whole thing collapsed. Needless to say, the robin flew away. We both laughed (the music of her laugh seemed to be better than any drugs they could pump into me), and then it was her turn. We switched off, each telling a story to counter the other, revealing more and more about each other in the process. At one point the doctor came in and took my pulse, but that was it. Finally we came to my reasons for being a cop.

"My brother Mort. I told you about him, right?" I had indeed. Mortimer had died in a boating 'accident' just off the coast. "Well, no one was ever convinced that it was an accident, least of all my mom. The cops didn't seem to care. They chalked it up to accident and would have left it at that except my mom pushed and pushed, constantly calling them until finally they looked into it a little deeper.

"They found some evidence that there had been something flammable on board, and they must have gotten some fingerprints or something, because the next thing we know they're hauling in some guy named Rizzoli and charging him with the murder. Well, there was a trial, and in the end the guy got off because the cops had mishandled one of the key pieces of evidence. It really pis... er... irked me that that could happen, and so I decided I could maybe make a difference." I took a moment to laugh at my idealism. Miss Emily was shaking her head slowly.

"That's so sad."

"I agree."

We looked at each other, and then something happened. She leaned in, and I stretched myself up, and our lips were on a collision course, and then the doctor came in, making a lot of noise. She backed off and I let my head fall. I turned and glared at him.

"Well, hello there."

He was an older guy, wrinkled and gray. He looked like my mental image of a grandfather, paternal in an ancient sort of way. This was the sort of man you could easily see yourself confiding in, anything from the key to an award winning garden to colon related discomfort, and it made him a rather unsettling guy.

"I see you're feeling a bit better."

"What's up, Doc?" I wrinkled my nose and gnashed my teeth, aiming for Bugs Bunny but getting a little closer to that guy from the cannibal movie. He chuckled.

"That's good. I'm gonna have to remember that." He busied himself checking my chart, and then looked at me again. "Well, son, you're awake, and that's really the only reason we had to keep you."

"So, I can leave?"

"Anytime you feel up to it." He scribbled something on the chart and then handed me a slip. "That's for some painkillers."

"For what?"

"The rib. I know you don't feel much now, but once the stuff we gave you wears off you'll think a piece of your side got ripped out by a gator." He winked at me and I nodded.

"Thanks."

"No problem." He left and I turned back to Miss Emily.

"Now where were we?"

"Getting ready to get you home." She had stood and was gathering her things. Drat. Her lips had looked so nice, too… Like elongated raspberries.

* * *

I dressed quickly and hobbled out through the door into the hall, where Miss Emily was waiting. She helped me to the elevator and out the door, then into her car. She took me first to the drugstore, then back to the apartments, and walked me to my door, only letting me go when I was safely inside. "Now, I don't want you leaving, ok? You need your rest. Doctor's orders." She promised to come back and cook me dinner later. I thanked her profusely and watched as she left. The chair was inviting, and I had no problems with relaxing in it.

I thought of many things, of Humpty and the other officers, of Ricky and the building, of the captain, and how old he seemed to have gotten in the last few days. I thought of Miss Emily. Never in my entire life would I have foreseen anything like this happening. She genuinely seemed to like me. It was a comfortable feeling, being liked. I thought of Mortimer, my brother, something I hadn't done in a long time. Ah, Mortimer.

It had all started as a missing persons case, oddly enough. See, one morning this hysterical mother mouse came into the station and demanded to see an officer. This was back before I was on the force. My brother, however, was there, and he was the one who got stuck with her. He had taken her into one of the back rooms and listened as she unfolded a very odd story.

"My son is missing, but I know where he is."

"Excuse me?"

"He's missing."

"Yes…"

"But I know where he is."

"Ok…"

"See, this is what happened." She folded her feet at the ankle and placed her bag on the ground next to her seat. "This man, a perfectly nice gentleman, came by a few days back and asked if we would be interested in watching a presentation on the benefits of music. Well, I was pretty sure he was trying to sell something, so I told him we weren't interested. He was awfully insistent, though, and so I invited him in.

"He said that it really didn't matter if we didn't buy anything, he just wanted the chance to give the presentation. He got paid for it either way, and it only took a half hour. Anyway, he started setting up in the living room and I went to get drinks. He asked for green tea. I remember that struck me as a little odd."

"Odd?"

"Yes. I find that when a gentleman asks for tea, he's either sick or one of those sinful, sinful homosexuals, and since he didn't sound sick, I immediately thought it must be the latter."

Mort had written that down. "Sorry. Please, continue."

"Alright. I went to get the drinks, and came back to ask him if he wanted any sugar for his tea. You know what I found him doing?"

"What?"

"He was entertaining my..." she gulped, "...my Stephen."

"Stephen is..."

"My son."

"Of course. So, he was entertaining your son?"

"With a watch!"

"A watch?"

"Yes, one of those dangling ones that men carry around in their pockets."

"A pocket watch?"

"No, it was on a chain."

"A pocket watch."

"No, it wasn't in his pocket."

"I know that, but that's what the watch is called. It's a style."

"I think it was a Rolex."

"I don't think Rolex makes pocket watches."

"It wasn't a pocket watch. It was a dangly watch."

"Alright. Alright. What kind really doesn't matter. What happened next?"

"Well, I asked him about the sugar and he said yes, the sweeter the better, which just proved to me even more that he was," she leaned forward and dropped her voice, "of a different sexuality." With the word sex her face turned a light shade of red.

"Asking for sugar makes a man gay?"

"Oh no, not gay. Sugar doesn't make anyone happy, only a tad loopy."

"So why did that make you think he was gay?"

"The way he said it." She acted it out, and Mort did indeed see what she meant.

"I see."

"Anyway, I got the tea things and brought everything out and we watched the presentation."

"We?"

"Stephen and I. I was actually a little surprised when he said he wanted to watch too, but what is a mother to do?"

"What was the presentation about?"

"Music camp."

"Music camp?"

"Yes. The man wanted me to send little Stephen away to a camp for several weeks. He said he could teach him to play the flute like an angel."

"In weeks?"

"He said he had invented a marvelous system, one that worked wonders."

"Really?"

"Yes. Anyway, the presentation was highly convincing, and Stephen informed me he fully intended to go."

"And you didn't like that idea, I take it?"

"It wasn't that I didn't like the idea. I believe that if a child wants to play a musical instrument, then he should be able to. I would have preferred he chose something that didn't involve all that sucking and blowing, but what is a mother to do?" She laughed awkwardly.

"Yes. So, what does this have to do with your son's disappearance?"

"Well. I told him that if he really wanted to he would have to come up with part of the money. We aren't poor, my dear, but we aren't rich either. The camp wasn't overly expensive, but it would have made quite a dent in our finances."

"So did he get the money?"

"Oh, he didn't have to."

"Excuse me?"

"He didn't have to. The man, who told us his name was Mr. Michaels, said that he had never seen someone so cut out for playing the flute as my Stephen, and that he would speak to the camp director about a possible scholarship."

"Wow. That's impressive."

"Yes, sir, well, my Stephen is impressive."

"So the scholarship came through?"

"Yes, and I took him to where the bus was supposed to leave myself."

"Supposed to leave?"

"Well, I didn't see a bus when I got there, but Mr. Michaels was waiting, and he told me that Stephen could wait in the building with him. The bus was a little late."

"And you just left?"

"Well, I hugged Stephen, gave him a phone card, and told him to call me every day. He didn't particularly care for that, but I insisted."

"And then you left?"

"Yes, then I left."

"And did he call?"

"Twice."

"Twice?"

"Yes. Once later that day to tell me that the bus had gotten there safe and once to tell me he wasn't too sure about the camp anymore."

"So why didn't you go to pick him up?"

"Well..." Here she got very quiet and slumped in the chair. "I kinda don't know where it is."

"What?"

"I don't know where the camp is."

"You sent your kid to a camp when you have no idea where it is?"

"I'm sorry. Sheesh. I don't know why I did it, just that I did. It's almost like I didn't have any real control over what I was doing." Mort had written that down as well.

"Ok, miss. If you'll just give your name and information to the man at the desk out there," he pointed out the door, "then you can leave."

"Ok." She stood and grabbed her bag. "You will find him, right officer?"

"Well, I can't promise you that. I can promise you I'll try. I can even tell you that the odds are good we'll find him. It doesn't really sound like there's anything really wrong here."

Turns out Mort was wrong. Within a week, something near ten other families had come in with approximately the same story. A man calling himself Mr. Michaels was going around signing kids up for some camp that apparently wound up not being as good as it was supposed to be and none of the parents knew where their kids were.

Every single missing person was a young mouse or rat, but what Mort found especially interesting was the first woman's story about the watch. She was the only one who mentioned anything like that, but all of the stories included an instance where the man was left alone with the kids.

To Mort this seemed key, but he couldn't quite put his finger on why. I can remember the night he came over for dinner and couldn't concentrate, even though mom had fixed his favorite dinner: take out Chinese. He mused over the case the entire time, talking about the missing kids over his moo-shoo pork, pondering the meaning of the watch over his fortune cookies, and wondering how it was that so many parents could be dumb enough to let their kids go off to camp without knowing where they were over ice cream (admittedly not Chinese, but the idea is the same).

My dad was trying to get him to relax, and so turned on the television, hoping to find a baseball game but instead tuning in a hypnotist. The guy was in the middle of a joke, and my dad decided it couldn't be too bad. My brother wandered in and sat down, and before too long they were both laughing uproariously. Then the guy hypnotized a man so he thought he was a chicken.

My brother sat straight up and his eyes opened wide. "Son, you ok?" My mom came out of the kitchen and looked in with worried eyes.

"Mort? Hon? You ok?"

"Shhh." His gaze was fixed on the television, and our heads all turned in unison to see what he was looking at. The man was now hopping around like a chicken, flapping his arms and trying his darndest to lay an egg. Mort jumped out of his seat and ran for the door. "I gotta go, Mom, Dad. Thanks for dinner." He was out the door before my mom could remind him to put on his shoes. The door had scarcely shut before he was back in, grabbing for them.

The sky had opened up and water was streaming down now, so Mort's feet were all wet. "Hehe. Forgot my shoes. Sorry." He was up again and out the door before my mom could say anything about his coat. Again, as soon as the door shut Mort was back. He grabbed his coat, then kissed my mom on the cheek and glanced once more at the television, where the man was now on one of the stools, squatting, darting his forward every few seconds and squawking. Then he was gone.

We watched as the car peeled out of the driveway, and then went back to what we had been doing. Mort drove off to the station and looked in his files to find the first lady's information. He then called her up, but there was no answer. Before the third ring, he slammed the phone down and ran back out to the car.

He reached her house a scant ten minutes later and pulled the car up to the curb in front of her door. He opened the door, pulled his coat over his head, and got out, slamming the door behind him and sprinting for the door. He made it about three feet before slipping in the mud and going down on his butt.

He hauled himself up, brushing at the wet mud that was now clinging to him, and continued toward the door, which he could now see was ajar. The frame was splintered, the door itself scuffed as though someone had kicked it in. Mort gulped and pulled his gun. After he pushed the door open, he yelled in. No one answered.

His foot was on the threshold when lightning flashed over head, illuminating the house and causing Mort to drop his gun, partly in fear and partly in revulsion. The living room was a disaster, and not because it hadn't been clean. There was blood everywhere, soaked into the walls and the carpet, pooled on the carpet and the couch, and even smeared over the television, which, oddly enough, was tuned to the exact same program Mort had been watching at the house just a half hour before. The thunder roared a few seconds later, and the noise pulled Mort back to reality. He sidestepped into the room and called out again. "Is there anyone here?"

He reached a lamp and used the end of his coat as a glove to twist the knob, turning it rapidly. The light came on, got brighter, and then went out again. He had turned it once too many times. He did it again, this time stopping on time, and then closed his eyes. His breath was coming in ragged gasps, and he was trying hard not to let his moo-shoo revisit the world of, well, not his stomach.

He opened his eyes slowly and confirmed that he had indeed seen it all. The blood was still there, the gore, and now he could see where it had come from. Well, part of where it had come from. There, at the foot of the television, was a foot of the rodent persuasion. On the foot was a fuzzy pink slipper, and the foot ended in a ragged stump about three inches above the ankle. The rest of the house seemed to be beckoning, but Mort decided he should probably get some backup first.

He staggered out the front door and was surprised to see a shadowy figure hunkered over his driver's side door. Just then the lightning came again, and he was able to make out the man's features. He looked up and saw Mort, and then sprinted off down the street. Mort, no slouch when it came to running, took off after him and the chase was on.

The guy got about halfway up the street, and then darted off down a narrow alleyway. Mort, who was by now closing the gap, followed him and leaped the trash-cans the man dumped over. The man reached the end of the alleyway and was confronted with a chain link fence. He didn't even hesitate, but jumped as high as he could and then scrambled the rest of the way to the top.

Mort was close enough that he could grab for the guy's foot, and he did just that, causing the guy to lose his balance and topple over the other side, flailing his arms. This turned out to be a horribly bad idea as the ring on his right hand caught on one of the spokes and all his weight was suddenly jerked back by his ring finger. This was obviously not something that should naturally happen, and his finger quickly realized that, ripping away from his hand with a sickening pop that Mort could hear clearly even over the sound of the pounding rain.

The man lay on the other side of the fence screaming, his body curled into the fetal position, and Mort shuddered. He reached through one of the holes in the fence and grabbed the man's other wrist. It came easily, and Mort slapped cuffs around it and the fence. He then went back to his car and radioed for help. Other officers converged on the scene within minutes, and Mort led them first to the man without a finger.

They undid the cuffs and helped him into an ambulance, and one of the medics took the finger off the fence, putting it on ice and handing the container into the vehicle. He then climbed in and off it went.

The rest of the night was spent going over the house. It turned out that the foot was, indeed, from the lady who had first come to Mort. Her body was found in the bedroom, in a similarly disassembled state. The murder weapon, a gas powered chainsaw, was found lying next to her, clumps of hair and other things drying on the still warm steel.

The blood was everywhere, and it was obvious that she had been put through pain. They wrapped up near dawn, and Mort headed off to the station to file his report. When he got there, though, he found something else waiting for him. The men at the hospital had filed their report and managed to find out who the guy was.

A Mr. Richard Michaels, the man was an exterminator by trade. He specialized in the destruction of annoying household pests of various sorts and was known to be particularly shady. The finger had not been saved (they tried, but by the time they actually got to it, the thing was gray and dead, and since no one on staff was related in any way to Frankenstein, the thing was abandoned and thrown in with the other biohazards, which were then shipped off to a local burger chain to be made into fast food. Well, not really, but that's what that crap tastes like sometimes), but he was expected to recover completely. They wanted Mort to get right over.

The techs from the house had found many fingerprints, and while they still had to process everything, there were at least three distinctly different sets. Mort was betting that one of the sets would match up with Mr. Michaels. He left the station and drove over to the hospital, where he parked his car and headed in. He had to wait around for nearly an hour before someone would see him (some sort of a mistake where they thought he was a patient in need of care. Once they realized he wasn't, they saw him immediately), but he was eventually taken up to the room.

Michaels was just waking up as Mort came in, and the other officers left the room. "Hey there, bug guy. How's the finger?"

"I dunno, you tell me." He held up a different finger, one that Mort wasn't overly fond of.

"Funny. I'm glad to see that your sense of humor wasn't overly affected."

"Bite me."

"Wow, witty, aren't we?"

"What do you want?"

"To talk. Why did you do it?"

"Do what?"

"Dress up in a tutu and dance the watusi. You know perfectly well what." He lowered his head and started laughing. At first it was alright, if a little odd, but before too long the laugh raised in pitch, and when he raised his head again, his eyes were rolled back in his head.

"I killed them! I killed them all!" His voice was much different, higher in pitch and somewhat gravelly. Mort started to feel a little queasy.

"You killed them?"

Instead of answering, the man laughed. "Blood... everywhere... blood. Screams. Ah, the music of it all. Scream, my pretties, scream!"

"Dude, you ok?"

"The life of the many for the life of the one." He laughed again, a high pitched near screech.

"What does that mean?"

"Mean? What does it mean? He wants to know what it means."

He stopped, as if listening, and then continued. "It means I will live…"
He stopped, and then his voice came out low and evil sounding. He
stretched the word out into several syllables. "Forever."

"Forever?"

"Forever." Back to the old voice, which was actually the new
voice, but not the newest, so it was old. "I will never die!" He broke
up laughing again, and Mort backed off. He paged a nurse with the
button on the wall and watched as the man writhed on the bed. The
nurse came in and screamed when she saw the man.

By this time he had managed to rip the stitches from his finger
and blood was spurting out. The i.v. was on its way out as well, and
the blood was beginning to well there. Mort jumped to the side of
the bed and held him down as best he could as the nurse pulled
straps from a drawer across the room and hooked them to the sides
of the bed. She pulled them tight across his chest and Mort moved to
his legs.

She started to put the straps on his legs and he kicked up, catching
her on the under side of the chin and shattering her jaw. She fell to
the ground, howling, and Mort was left holding one leg while the
other flopped like a dead fish. Then, suddenly, it stopped. He
cautiously let go of the leg he had been holding, and it fell to the
bed, perfectly still. He found the man's wrist and felt for a pulse.
There was none.

The nurse was screaming, partly from fear but mainly from pain,
and Mort was about to page again when several nurses, a doctor, and
the other cops came into the room. The doctor moved immediately
to the nurse, and one of the nurses moved to the bed. She felt for a
pulse on the neck and, finding none, pulled back his eyelid. The eyes
were still rolled back in his head but now the white had been replaced
with red, sacks of blood that would no longer see the world. The
bleeding from the finger had slowed and she grabbed the hand.
Nothing.

She turned back to help the others with the nurse on the floor,
and Mort turned to the other men. "Ok, guys. We have to find these
kids. I have a very bad feeling that this is not going to end up alright."

The other men left, heading for the station to find the address for the building the first woman had taken her kid to. Mort stuck around until the doctor pronounced Michaels dead, and then he headed out. He was in the car when the radio crackled and one of the officers he had sent back came on with the address. Mort told them to get over there, that he would meet them, and then headed over himself.

He reached the place just as the other cars pulled in. It was a warehouse by the docks, and as he stepped out he could smell the sea air. As he related the story later, he never expected what they found. He had thought it would be bad, had steeled himself for the worst, and yet it still shattered him. I remember when he told us, several hours later, about the approach to the doors, about the overpowering odor of iron and dank. I remember my dread as he related kicking open the door and rushing in, his gun aimed straight ahead of him, and I especially remember how it took him three tries to finally tell what he saw.

At this point, I think I've blocked most of what he said about the scene out of my memory. It was that gruesome. What I do remember is that the kids were all there, and that they were not alive. Mort said he hoped they had died before what happened to them happened, and I had to agree. Once the fingerprints were run, it was found that the third set did indeed belong to Mr. Michaels. They also found his prints all over the warehouse.

During the investigation, they found that he had been seeing a shrink for several months. The psychiatrist was a guy named Rizzoli. If Mort had just let things alone at that point, then he might still be alive. Instead, he decided that it was very important that he see Michaels' file. Rizzoli told him he couldn't find it, and Mort thought that was a little strange. He demanded to see it, and Rizzoli said he might have it at his house, that he could have it the next day.

Well, Mort went back and saw him the next day, got a good look at the file. Michaels had been certifiably insane for nearly a year. When Mort asked Rizzoli why he hadn't done anything about it, he just claimed ignorance. How was he to know that Michaels would kill? He had seemed perfectly harmless.

Well, Mort wasn't too happy about that, and so he got an investigation started into Rizzoli's background. It turned out that he had connections to the King (a cousin of some sort), and that there were some shadier things in his past, including a speculated mob connection. What was really interesting was that Michaels had connections to the same mob.

After a little digging, Mort found that Rizzoli had been a sort of mob recruiter, finding people to do dirty work, and that they had gotten him a job as a shrink specifically for that purpose. What Mort speculated was that Rizzoli would find people who were nearly crazy, or at least susceptible to the idea of 'dirty' work, and then would exploit them. He figured that Michaels was an irresistible find and that Rizzoli had recruited him without understanding the true depths of his dementia.

Mort called the house one day to say that he was going to be late to dinner. He had gotten a tip that there was some sort of a deal going on down by the docks and he had to check it out. That was the last time we ever heard his voice. When he was two hours late, Mom called the station trying to find out what was going on. I was sitting in the living room watching television, and when she started screaming I nearly spilled my soda (not that it would have made much of a difference since the couch was already stained beyond recognition).

Mort was dead. He had been at the docks investigating a tip and had somehow wound up on a boat that exploded. Divers found the wreckage of the boat he had been on. Since he had called in the fact that he was going out in the boat, they chalked it up to some sort of mishap. As suspicious as it seemed, they had no reason to believe there had been anyone else on the boat. Besides, they had just about given up on the Rizzoli link by then.

Well, Mom was wicked angry about the whole thing. She found it disgusting that they weren't going to make someone pay, to find a killer, and so she kept the pressure up, calling the station all the time and just being a general nuisance. They eventually decided to appease her and made a more thorough investigation of the boat's wreckage.

What they found surprised everyone. There were traces of accelerant in the wood of the boat, stuff that hadn't quite burnt up. That led to a more in-depth investigation of the whole thing, and they eventually did find a witness who was able to place Rizzoli at the scene. They brought him in and one of the cops got a little overzealous and knocked the guy around.

Well, he let his lawyer in on that when he got there, and when the thing went to trial he brought it out as proof of the treatment of his client. The judge didn't want to buy it, but he had no choice. That and the fact that the accelerant turned out to be ordinary gasoline, something that shouldn't have been there but could easily be explained away, led to his acquittal. I was so mad about the whole thing that I decided that I wanted to be a cop, and when I turned twenty-one I signed on. I've been here ever since.

Anyway, I sighed and reclined in the chair, raising the leg cushion and pushing back on the top. The ceiling was staring back at me now, covered in patterns from the light shining through the windows, and I could hear a bird singing somewhere. Everything seemed almost right in the world, as if nothing bad could ever happen and the light airy feeling of happiness was all that you could ever need.

Of course, then I decided to take a deep breath and that ruined the entire moment. Searing pain ripped into me and I was grateful for having gotten Miss Emily to stop and let me get the pain pills. I sat up, slowly, and made my way to the counter, where I had put the medicine bottle. As I passed the door, I noticed that there was an envelope on the floor.

In my condition I couldn't very well lean over and grab it, so I thought about how to reach the thing, finally settling on a piece of tape stuck to my shoe. I stepped on the envelope and brought my leg up within reach of my hands, grabbing it and the tape from my shoe. The handwriting looked vaguely familiar, and I couldn't place it at first. Then I realized it was addressed in the same hand as the sympathy card I had received after Humpty's death.

I slowly tore it open and pulled the paper out. "Dear John," it began. If my heart hadn't suddenly decided to try and run a marathon,

I probably would have laughed. "First off, I would like to commend you. I'd like to think I could be that cool under pressure. Secondly, I'd like to let you know a little secret." The print got smaller, almost as thought the writer expected me to see it as whispering. Oddly enough, that's exactly how I read it.

"The bomb wasn't set to a timer. I waited until I knew you were clear, and then let it go." Suddenly the writing was back to the old size. "You may ask why, but I think it's something you need to figure out for yourself. Best wishes on a speedy recovery, John." There was no signature, although I had a fairly good idea of who had written it.

Why would Jack want me to get Ricky? The only reason I could possibly fathom was that Ricky was a decoy, and the more I thought about it, the more the idea made sense. Ricky was handed over because the information he could give us was wrong. That way we could be manipulated into looking elsewhere while Jack and his "goons" built up their plan. I was going to reach for the phone when I decided just to head down there myself. It felt bad to go out after I told Miss Emily I wouldn't, and so I came up with a good reason in my head. My car. I needed my car.

* * *

I had to call a taxi to take me down, but I got there. On the way past my desk I heard a loud commotion, and I made my way toward the sound (Brad Henshaw's desk) to see a girl of about seventeen and three bears, a small one, a middle one, and a big one. They were all talking excitedly and Brad was having difficulty getting the entire story. "Yo!" The talking ceased. "Ok, how's about we start over, one at a time, ok? You there, Goldilocks, you start."

"Alright." She turned her nose up at the bears and I knew instantly that she was the kind of girl I had detested in high school. Her 'daddy' was probably rich, or at least well off, and she had most likely never hurt for anything, which, to her mind, made her something special. Hot stuff. People like her had made my high school experience suck, because I was always the one no one wanted to be around, and the popular kids, like her, I assumed, always thought it was hilarious to pick on me and... I stopped myself. That didn't matter.

"I was walking along and saw some smoke coming out of one of the windows in this big old run down house, so I decided to go tell them." Her voice had taken on a tone of righteous indignation, as if having to explain herself was an inexcusable affront. "I got up to the front door and knocked, and the door opened up by itself. I headed in and went around calling for them, but no one was around, so I went up and put the fire out."

The biggest cut in. "Bull." Brad glared at him. "Sorry."

"Continue." Brad seemed to enjoy the one word commands.

She glanced around nervously, and then continued. "Well, I was walking away and I slipped on some of the water I had used to put the fire out, smacked my head on a bedpost and the next thing I know these friggin' bears are standing around me actin' all pissed off and now I'm here."

"Ok." Brad turned to the bears. "What do you say happened?"

"Well, we were all set to sit down to lunch when Junior there realized he had left his baseball mitt down by the park." The kids played baseball down in the park when it was nice out. I had never understood the appeal of baseball. It all seemed to boil down to a bunch of guys standing around in a field getting paid more per minute than I would ever make in a day. To tell you the truth, it always seemed like I might as well be watching stockbrokers at work. Probably would be more fun, too.

"So we all got in the minivan and headed down. He got the glove and we went back. I was the last one in the kitchen and Momma was looking at the food."

"Someone had been nibbling at my steak." The mother apparently liked her steak a lot, because she said this with a spark of vehemence. The father spoke again.

"Yea, and someone had nibbled at mine too. Poor Junior's was completely gone." The poor kid looked like he might cry. "Well, I was afraid someone might still be in the house, so I grabbed the bat and we walked into the living room."

"Someone was sitting in my chair!" The mother practically shrieked this. Brad looked at Goldi. The father started again.

"Not at that exact moment. See, she's got this thing about pillows, right? And the three chairs always got pillows on 'em." This sounded like it had been an issue between them for some time, and by explaining he was somehow winning an argument. "She can tell when any of 'em have been moved at all. Someone had been in my chair too. Junior's chair was friggin' broken."

The kid seriously seemed to be on the verge of some sort of breakdown, and the father showed no signs of letting up. "So finally we headed upstairs and found this little…" He glanced at his wife and kid, and then changed his mind. "This kid in Junior's bed." Junior didn't seem to be too upset about the fact that there had been a girl in his bed, but who could really blame him? Brad looked from the bears to Goldilocks, and back again.

"So, do you wanna press charges?"

"Heck yea I do," the father roared. I decided to take off. Technically I wasn't even supposed to be there in the first place, and I had to find my car and get back, 'cause Miss Emily was coming at 6:30 to cook dinner.

VIII. Chicken Little

I tapped on the captain's door and slowly eased my way in after hearing what sounded like a grunt of assent. The captain was on the phone, and he gave me an odd questioning look as I entered. He spoke quickly, in lowered tones. "Yea, look. I gotta go. We'll hash the rest of this out tonight, ok?" Again he listened.

"Well, see if you can't hold off, ok? Just give me a few more hours." After listening a little bit more, he uttered an obscenity that I personally tend to avoid, slammed the phone down and looked up at me. "John? What're you doin' here? You're supposed to be down at the hospital."

"Well, they let me go. I'm supposed to be back home now, but I decided I needed my car. Actually, I kinda wanted to talk to you anyway." He seemed to mull this over, then motioned with one hand to the chair in front of his desk. Again I was struck by how old he looked. The past few days had been trying ones for him, as I well knew. I couldn't help thinking, though, as I lowered myself gratefully into the chair, that something seemed to be wrong. At times it was easy to forget I was currently sporting a busted rib, and at others it was utterly impossible. This was one of those impossible times.

"How can I help ya, John?" He folded his hands in front of him and made a face that was supposed to convey intentness but instead verged on exhausted disparity.

"Well, it's this Jack Henry business." I was pleased to see that he perked his head up. "I got a card in the mail the day after Humpty…" I stopped, looking him in the eyes, but I decided he knew what I was gonna say, and that actually vocalizing the words was unnecessary.

"Anyway, it was a condolence card. Actually, come to think of it, that shouldn't have gotten there so fast… I mean, the postal guys are fast, but geez…" I trailed off, thinking, and it took a polite cough from across the desk to pull me out of it. "Sorry. Must be the drugs."

"I don't want to sound rude, but can you get to the point?" He was waiting for the Jack Henry connection.

"Yea. It was a condolence card and I didn't realize it at the time, but it came from Jack Henry. You know all the stuff that's been going on." I quickly explained everything, and then told him about the new card, finishing with my suspicions that Ricky was a decoy. "And so here's my hunch." I looked at him again. The captain seemed to have been truly drawn in by my story, absorbed in every word I was letting loose. "I think Henry wants to do something during the King's visit." The captain flinched, then sat back.

"This…" He faltered, but then seemed to collect himself. "This is really bad news."

"I agree. What should we do?"

"Well, if it really is the King's visit, then we've got three days. I think we should pump Ricky until he tells us the truth."

"But what if he is a decoy?"

"Listen." His voice got harder, growing an edge I hadn't realized existed in the Captain. "Ricky is the only link we have to this guy. We need to know where he is. Whether he's a decoy or not, he has to know something. All we have to do is push until we get to the truth."

I almost said something about how we wouldn't really be able to tell the truth from the lies, but instead sighed and let my shoulders drop. He was right, after all. Ricky was our only link, and we had to press any advantage we could get. "And you aren't to come anywhere near this station until the end of the week." That one knocked the wind out of me.

"What?" I managed to gasp the word out, but even as I did I realized the truth. Not only was I too involved in the case, but I had also been wounded. Rather badly, I remembered as the rib began to throb again. Never gasp when you have a broken rib. It hurts. A lot. Like being kicked in the groin by a leg obsessed weightlifter, only in the rib area instead.

"I think you know why. Now go. Get outta here." He shooed me

her on the head. *Holy crap*, she thought, looking up at the sky. Now, this was a very cloudy day, and when she looked up she managed to catch a very fleeting glimpse of the open air through the clouds above her. That was enough to convince her that the sky, or some part of it, was falling. I told you she was a woman. Sheesh. Ok, so maybe I'm not as politically correct as I thought, but I can play a mean blues guitar, so it all kinda evens out.

Anyway, she decided that everyone needed to know that the sky was falling and ran off to tell as many people as she could. The results were kinda weird. Everyone seemed to believe her, from the little kids to the grown adults. Rich, poor, white, black, man, woman... The insane idea appealed to everyone, for some reason, and it spread faster than perfume in a brick, uh, crapper.

Eventually there was a huge crowd outside the King's palace, demanding some sort of action be taken. The King, who hadn't been raised a fool, basically called them all numbskulls for believing such a stupid idea, and they decided the wisest course of action was to riot. The police had to step in (with full riot gear, mind you) and bash a few skulls, but it all got settled pretty quickly. The mob mentality was a strong one indeed, and the last thing we needed was to kick off another riot. Thus, the situation needed to be handled with extreme delicacy.

I was completely absorbed in these thoughts, so when I heard seagulls I was very confused and snapped back to reality in order to look around. We were nowhere near the central lot. In fact, we seemed to have headed in the exact opposite direction. I leaned forward and knocked on the glass partition.

"Yo." The cabbie didn't acknowledge me. "Yo, cabbie." Still nothing. I decided to press on. "You're goin' the wrong way. The lot is back there." I jerked my thumb behind me and still the driver in no way acknowledged me. "Son of a..." I reached into my pocket and pulled out my badge. "Hey, pal. I'm a cop. You better stop this friggin car right now." Again, nothing. Fine.

I reached down and pulled on the handle. Nothing. I tried to lift the lock and only then noticed that there wasn't one. "What the heck is goin' on here?" I was getting a little bit frightened now. "Yo." I said it slowly, deliberately, stretching it into two syllables.

Still nothing, so I spun around until my feet were pointed at the window on the left, then pulled back and kicked as hard as I could. Nothing, except for a shooting pain through my side. Also, my breath decided that was a good time to desert me. "Aww crap," I choked out, grabbing at my chest and laying on my side.

Still nothing. That's when I decided the best idea was probably to just let whatever happened happen, and worry about it later. That particular action plan seemed fine to me, and my mind was firmly set on just paying attention and waiting for the right chance. My body, on the other hand, decided that it was a great time to take a little rest, and I blacked out.

* * *

Even before I opened my eyes I could feel the ropes pulling into my wrists. I was sitting on a chair of some sort and my hands were quite tightly bound behind me. Slowly I let my eyes open, suddenly certain I wasn't going to like what I saw, and as it turned out I was right. Directly in front of me was a table, and sitting on the table, at eye level, was a head staring right at me.

The head didn't blink for the longest time, and I very slowly realized that it was just a head, one with no body left. The worst part (and when seeing a disembodied head isn't the worst part of the whole situation, you know something is bad) was that I recognized the head. It was Roscoe. Or, it had been Roscoe.

I had to struggle to keep from letting some of the choicer contents of my stomach fly and closed my eyes tightly, steeling myself against what I knew was there, and turned my head before opening them again. I was seated about twenty yards away from a very large wall, which met, if I craned my neck up, a roof about forty feet up, all of which helped me to decide I was in a warehouse somewhere near the docks.

Turning my head in the other direction (and closing my eyes again when I passed Roscoe's head), I looked to the other side, where I saw some boxes and a large machine with arms, one of those pallet moving jobbies. Suddenly I realized that my head hurt. A lot.

It was like some crazed construction worker was in my brain, hammering away with an industrial sized jackhammer. Or maybe it was like those thousands of monkeys working on *Hamlet*. Or maybe… I forced myself to snap out of it. This was no time for going off the deep end. Concentration was the key, I found, and I started trying to figure out more about where I was.

As far as I could tell, there was no one in the room besides the gruesome visitor in front of me and myself. Somewhere far off I heard waves, and closer was a dripping sound. Just as I was getting used to my surroundings (and deciding that it was more like one of those hammer games at the fair, where you had to ding the bell to win a prize, only about fifty times worse), they changed. Well, the sounds did anyway. First there was a flushing noise, and then water running.

A door clanged open somewhere behind me and footfalls crossed the floor and stopped behind me. "You up?" The voice was gruff. I didn't answer. "I said," he said, "you up?" As if to emphasize the word "up", he hit me in the back of the head with something quite hard. This wasn't very comfortable for me, especially considering the headache I was currently suffering through.

"Yes! Alright? Yes, I'm up."

He grunted. "Good." He then walked off again. I heard him cross to somewhere behind the boxes and dial a phone. He waited, and then spoke. "Yea, he's up." He listened. "Well, I had to prod him a little, but I think he's fine." He listened again. "Alright." The phone clicked down and I could hear him coming back. He stood behind me again. "I'm supposed to keep you company for a bit. The boss'll be here in a few." I heard something scrape forward, and then heard him settle down. It musta been a chair.

I struggled to find something to say. "Well, ya got me." It was pretty lame, but I never said I was a genius.

"True dat." I suddenly thought that the gruffness was fake. In fact, I could almost place the voice.

"So, as long as I'm here anyway, how about telling me a story?"

"Why, you scared?" He thought that was funny.

"I was thinkin' more a story about this. About what the heck is goin' on."

"Mmmm…" He was thinking. "Alrighty. Once upon a time there was a nosey cop. He upset the wrong guy, and then he got taken care of and he wasn't around no more. The end. Happy?" Apparently this guy had never told bedtime stories to little kids. Where was the action? Where was the intrigue? Where was the part where the cop didn't actually die?

"Not really. Come on, man. You know just as well as I do that the odds are I'm not makin it outta here."

"This is true."

"So? Why can't you tell me?"

"If you're gonna die either way, then what's the harm in my telling you, right?"

"Right."

"Well, if you're gonna die anyway, then what's the harm in my not telling you?" I didn't have an answer for that one. "That's what I thought." That's when I realized who it was.

"Harvey?" I heard a sharp intake of breath. "Harvey, what the heck are you doing?" It sounded like he stood up.

"How'd you know it was me?" Now his voice was back to normal.

"Hey, you got your secrets, I got mine."

"Aww great." He sounded upset, but then sighed, I think in an effort to calm down. "It doesn't matter. You ain't getting outta here alive anyway." He pulled his chair forward and sat a little off to the side, so I could see him and he could see me, and neither of us had to look at Roscoe's head.

"How could you, Harv? I've been nothing but nice to you."

"Nice? You call making me snitch nice? Do you know what happens to snitches?" I had a feeling I did, and involuntarily glanced at Roscoe's head in recognition of that fact. "Besides," he said, "I'm getting some nice money outta this. You gotta believe I liked money way before I ever liked you." I did believe it.

"But Harvey…" He just smiled back. I'd never noticed it before, but Harvey had quite a sinister smile, one packed with a lot of teeth.

"That's a lotta teeth you got there, Harv."

"All the better to eat you with…" He never finished. A gunshot cracked the air and he was suddenly slumping off to the side, a small hole in his head dribbling red. I did not want to see the back of his head, and I really didn't have to since I could still see a fine mist of blood floating where he had been.

The shot echoed off the walls for a long time, and as it finally faded away I caught the sound of footsteps from behind me. Jack Henry strode up and grabbed Harvey's chair, turning it around so he could sit down and rest his arms on the headpiece. He was holding a gun.

"John, John, John… You just can't leave well enough alone, can you?" He cocked his head, making me think rather involuntarily of a puppy looking for a treat. "I gave you a chance. Heck, I gave you a present. A friggin present!" He lost his cool for just a second and then seemed to regain some composure. "I gave you Ricky."

"And told him to lie." The words were out before I thought about it.

"Well, no. We just didn't tell Ricky the truth. Same thing in the end, I guess. But you weren't supposed to know that. I guess you're just a little too smart for your own good." He picked up the gun and aimed it at my head, then seemed to think better of it. "Ok, do you really want to know what's going on?" I nodded. Anything to buy some time.

He sighed, and then put his arms down again. "Well, someone, and I won't tell you who simply because I don't know exactly, is financing a little operation here. We're going to try and kill the King when he comes to visit. Nothing like a little insurrection to lift your spirits, eh?"

"Wait, how can you not know who's financing it?"

"Ahh… That's simple. I've been around a little too long to make a mistake like having any direct contact with the financer." He looked down at Harvey's corpse. "Looks like I won't be getting in touch with him very much anymore at all." Harvey was the link, then. "In fact, the absolute most I'll ever do is talk to the financer on the phone, and even then only on my special little friend." He opened a flap of his coat and I saw a cell phone peeking out of his breast pocket.

"So, you've never met the person?"

"Nope. I know it's a guy. That's about it."

"And you never get curious?"

"Oh, all the time. But, I'm a lot more worried about jail than I am curious about my backer, so it's all good. Now, I think I'm going to have to cut our chat short. I have some pressing business elsewhere." He again raised the gun.

Now, when a body dies, there is a point when the remaining life gives itself up. The life, of course, is stored gasses, muscles that had been tightened loosening, that sort of thing. I believe it's been called a death rattle in times past, but I don't know the technical term.

Whatever you call it, Harvey's body chose that precise instant to let it all go. The sudden noise (and it did indeed sound like a rattle) spooked Jack, and he glanced away from me, pointing the gun at the ceiling.

I had discovered during this whole thing that whoever bound my feet had neglected to do the same with my feet. That's a big no-no. Preparedness is important, folks. I kicked out as fast as I could and knocked Jack's chair over, sending him sprawling on his back. He wasn't expecting it, and thus let the gun go. It flew about ten yards closer to the wall. I steeled myself, knowing that I was about to get hurt, hoping that my chair was the same was Harvey's, and then stood and threw myself backwards, hard.

I lucked out and had a wooden chair as well, and when I landed it splintered. Laying dazed for just a second, I realized I was able to stand up, which I did, struggling since my hands were still bound behind me. Jack, behind me now, had landed on his back and lay there for a second, either trying to comprehend what had just happened or struggling to get his breath back, or maybe both. Heck, maybe he bashed his head and was seeing a big green Martian with white teeth. I don't know what he was doing, but when I turned I saw him struggling to his feet, and then looking wildly for the gun.

He saw me just as I saw the gun, and he followed my gaze. First he saw the gun, and then he was sprinting for it. As soon as I had seen the gun I was up and sprinting as well, and we reached the gun at nearly the same instant. I decided it would be more beneficial to me if I could keep him away from the gun simply because there was no way I would have been able to fire it, and threw myself into him, effectively throwing both of us down into a huddled mess.

I rolled on my stomach and was standing up again when a fist connected with my face. I looked up, blinking through pain, and saw Jack's face had been nicely scratched up. He even had a dollop of blood near his forehead. "Oh, you're gonna pay for that," he said, reaching into a pocket and pulling out a knife. "You're gonna pay a lot."

With that, I turned and ran off towards the boxes. I could hear him shouting with rage as he chased me, thankfully forgetting about the gun. He must have wanted to feel the kill this time, the blood, but that wasn't something I wanted to think at the time. Instead I reached the boxes and turned to see where he was. Jack was coming up at me pretty quick, the knife held out in front of him like some sort of skewer, and he lunged at me. I feinted to the side and heard the knife connect with wood.

"Crap!" He was trying to pull the knife out of the wood, but it didn't want to come. I kicked him, hard, in the hip and watched as he staggered to the side, swearing almost unintelligibly, and then fell in a heap. I kicked at the knife, knocking it out of the wood, and knelt over it, picking it up behind my back and using the blade to saw through the ropes on my wrists. Jack slowly pulled himself up, glaring at me.

"You're gonna die very slowly now. I was gonna be nice. I was gonna let you die quickly, with dignity. Now I'm gonna make you scream for your mommy. I'm gonna make you beg me to finish you off." He was staggering forward as he said this, and then reached for the knife. "First, however…" He stopped. The knife was gone.

"Looking for something?" I was still kneeling, and I held up the knife, handle first.

"Aww crap." I flicked the knife and it sank deep into his shoulder. He cried out and pulled at it, drawing it out slowly and watching, apparently in fascination, as blood seeped out. I didn't stick around to see it. Instead, I scrambled over to the gun and picked it up, aiming at Jack. "You friggin…" He finished with a very bad word, one I've decided I don't care to repeat (it was more a string of obscene words and suggestions with the word monkey thrown in periodically), and then rushed me, again with the knife out. I guess his rage and pain kinda blacked out his better sense.

"Dude… Dude, you don't wanna do this." He didn't seem to hear me, and when he reached about five yards away from me I pulled the trigger, hitting him in about the same place he had nailed Harvey. His body crashed into mine, the knife finding a home in my left shoulder, though I didn't notice it then. I looked into his eyes as he slid down. They were glazed over, and I could tell he was at least a little surprised. I stepped, shakily, over the body at my feet and walked to the boxes. I knew there was a phone back there somewhere, and I was right.

I dialed 911 and waited for the operator to pick up. "Hello, 911."

"Hey. This is John Monroe. I'm a police officer, and I need to report a crime."

"Ok, sir. Where are you?"

"I don't know."

"You don't know?"

"It's a warehouse, somewhere by the docks."

"Well, I'm afraid I'm going to need a little more than that." That's when I remembered the boxes. Maybe there would be an address on one. I told the operator to hang on and walked over to the closest box, to my relief blocking the carnage from my view. I looked all over the box and finally found what I was looking for. I ripped the label off the box and limped over toward the phone again.

"Hey piggy." I froze. "Aww… Is the po' widdle piggy scared?" I looked over toward where Jack had fallen and found, as I feared, he was no longer there. "Ahh. Yes. Where am I, John? Where am I? It's kinda tough to shoot something you can't see, isn't it?"

I turned to where it sounded like the voice was coming from, and was not too surprised to see a stack of boxes arranged in rows. I put the packing slip in my pocket and made my way over to the boxes, keeping the gun aimed in front of me. "Jack, just come out quietly. The cops will be here soon. There's nowhere you can go."

"Who says I want to go anywhere?" The left. "I know I'm as good as dead. I just want to make sure you are too." I had reached the boxes and saw a trail of blood heading off to the left.

"You're bleeding, Jack."

"You shot me, John. What do you think happens when you shoot someone?"

"That's not the point. You need medical attention."

"Oh, I have no intention of living. I know I'm as good as dead because I have every intention of killing myself when I'm done with you." I was getting closer.

"How are you gonna do that, Jack?"

"What do you mean?"

"How are you gonna kill me? I have the gun."

"So?" I was very close now.

"So, if I see you, you know I'll shoot you. You won't have a chance to kill me."

"Oh, I wouldn't be so sure." There, in front of me, behind the boxes.

"Then how are you gonna kill me, Jack?" No answer. "Jack?" That's when the boxes started to fall. The stack in front of me tilted forward and the top boxes were already sliding off. The first crashed down mere inches from my leg, and I backpedaled quickly. The boxes all fell and there was Jack, using a crowbar on the bottom box. As I realized what he was doing, he got it open and grabbed a gun from the stack inside.

"Bring it, piggy."

I steeled myself and dove to the side just as he pulled the trigger and a hail of bullets flew through the air I had recently occupied. I dragged myself behind the box I was lying against and ran through my options. He had a gun. A powerful one, apparently. The first thought I had was what he was doing with an automatic, the second was about where he was at that point. I slowly peeked around the edge of the box and saw that he was no longer there, so I scurried out and across the row, hiding behind a box on the other side.

"Here, piggy piggy." He was taunting me. "I just want to talk. Me and my friend Uzi. I'm not much of a talker, but that's ok. Uzi loves to chat." It sounded like he was heading up the row I had just been in, headed to where he had seen me go. I stood and tiptoed my way back up the row, heading away from him. I knew when he reached where he thought I was, because he swore and started taunting me again.

"C'mon, man. Tell ya what. If you come out now, I'll let it be painless again." I had reached the end of the row and was looking at a solid wall. To my left was a narrow corridor between a box and the wall. To the right was a ladder up to a walkway. I heard a grunt of anger behind me, and then a box toppled over. "Where are you?!?"

I pushed the boxes to the left of me back slightly, then kicked at the bottom one to make the whole pile wobble. I then climbed up the ladder as fast as I could. As I reached the top, the pile went, spilling boxes and more guns all over the floor. I ducked out of sight as Jack came running up, firing blindly at the mess, hoping to nail me in a soft and vulnerable place. He reached the pile and kicked at the debris. When he realized I wasn't there (dead or alive) he swore again. "Where are you, piggy? I'm getting sick of this." He took off back up the row, apparently missing the ladder, and I looked around.

The platform I was on ran the width of the building, starting from where I was and continuing to the other side, where a loading crane protruded through the wall. I started to shuffle my way toward the crane, trying to be as quiet as I could. By now I could hear the very faint sound of sirens. The operator must have gotten a trace on the call. Henry must have heard it too, because his voice got even louder.

"We'd better get this done with, piggy. Pretty soon all our fun will be over." He pushed another stack of boxes over and this time yelled out in surprise. "Looky what I got here." I got on my knees and looked over the edge. Jack had found a stockpile of grenades. He was in the process of grabbing a few. "Ok, piggy. If you don't come out, then I'll just wait for your friends to get here. Let's see how many of the other piggies I can take out, huh?" I backed up and stood against the wall.

If the others got here and he was still alive, then Jack wouldn't hesitate to pull the pins and let them take him. Then they'd all be dead. I needed to take care of him, and quick. I made my way to the edge again and aimed the gun at Jack's back. I tried to chamber a round silently, so as not to alert him, but he heard something, because he whirled around, bring his gun up, and opened fire.

I dove back, but not in time to avoid a bullet to the arm, almost in the exact same place as the knife wound from earlier. My arm was burning now, and the world was spinning.

"I'm comin for ya, piggy." He took off running toward the ladder, and I tried to pull it together. I struggled to my feet and started shambling toward the crane. Behind me, I heard Jack coming up the ladder. As I reached the crane, I heard his feet land on the platform. "Freeze, piggy."

I froze, but not before noticing the crane control lying on the ground about a foot in front of me. I looked up and saw the hook dangling about ten feet above me, then down over the edge of the platform. The distance from here to the ground was about the same as the GW bridge, which seemed oddly fitting.

"Ok, Jack. You got me." I heard him making his way along the walkway, and I put my hands over my head, shifting my weight and letting my left foot rest on top of the control. He reached me and pressed the gun to my head.

"No more running, piggy. I'm going to kill you now."

"Wait."

"What?"

"Why kill me?"

"Because I'm pissed at you. Because I know I'm not leaving here alive, and I want to take someone out with me. Because I hate you.

Take your pick."

"Why not just do what you were gonna do before?"

"What, blow people up?"

"Yea. I mean, if you can take out more people, why not, right?"

"Hey. You're right. Why not?" He reached down and took my gun. "Here's what I'm gonna do, piggy." He tossed the gun over the side and reached into his pocket, where he had stashed the grenades. When he pulled his hand out, he had one of the green balls, and he used his fingers to pull the pin. By now, the sirens were close enough that we could hear the wheels screeching as the vehicles stopped. Before too long, they would be entering the building. I had to do something now.

His arm was now around my neck, holding the grenade in front of my face. "I think I'll wait 'til they get up here, and then I'll let it go. Whaddya think of that, piggy?" I didn't say anything, just lowered my head in what I hoped was a posture of acquiescence. "Good little piggy." That's when I stomped on the down button.

The hook came whistling down and slammed Jack on the shoulder, knocking him to the floor. I had grabbed his hand right before the hook connected, so now I was holding his hand closed around the grenade. I used my other hand to raise the hook to a level just over the railing, and then grabbed hold of the control. Jack was stirring now, and I knew I only had one shot. I pulled the grenade from Jack's hand and held it in my hand. He was now fully awake again, and when he saw me he growled.

"Oh, that is it. Now you die, pig." He lurched to his feet and I threw my free arm over the hook. He dove at me and I sidestepped, shoving the grenade down the back of his pants as he passed.

"Happy trails, freak." I threw my other hand around the hook and pushed off to the side. I then hit the down button and the hook fell toward the ground. Above me I heard Jack scream out, and then I was rolling. I landed on my butt and looked up as Jack, in a desperate attempt to get at the grenade, lost his balance and fell off the walkway.

He got about halfway before the grenade went off. The concussion knocked me onto my back, and I lay there dazed as little bits of dust, ash, and Jack landed all around me. My ears were ringing quite badly, and my arm was burning as if it were being used to stoke a fire, but all in all I was alive and well, which is a lot more than I could say for Jack.

I didn't hear the medics when they came in, but the next thing I knew I was being loaded onto yet another stretcher. The tech team was walking around with dusting equipment, and a guy in a yellow suit was using a sponge to clean up what could only be blood. A few others were cataloguing the equipment from the boxes.

The captain was there, looking very sad, and the media was swarming just outside the doors. I contemplated calling out to the captain but decided that was a little pointless. After all, it was all done, right? I convinced myself that it would be fine if I were to just put my head down, and then the darkness overwhelmed me yet again.

IX. Baa Baa Black Sheep

I was really beginning to hate waking up in hospitals. Seriously. By this time I woulda thought that they'd have a dedicated room just for me, or maybe they woulda bumped me up to the presidential suite. Of course, that's assuming hospitals have presidential suites. I guess a presidential suite in a hospital would be like getting the extra large meal when you drive through somewhere: it's good, but it's overkill. Besides, wasn't everyone jumping on the extra large bandwagon these days? I made a mental note to check on the presidential suite.

This time when I woke up I was alone, which was both good and bad. I figured that if Miss Emily would come when the two of us weren't really all that close, then when we were close she would probably try even harder to get in and see me. Since Miss Emily wasn't there, then she must have been mad at me. That went beyond bad. In fact, it skated right past not cool and crash-landed directly into sucked.

The good part, the upside, was that I wouldn't have to worry about showing her too much of my backside when I got up. Stupid hospital gowns. You'd think that in this age of technological innovation someone would be able to come up with something better than the hospital gown. I mean, really. They might as well issue Speedos at the door for all the good those stupid things do.

It slowly dawned on me that not only was Miss Emily absent, but not one member of staff seemed to have noticed I was awake. At first I was a little upset by that, but then I decided it was for the best, since it meant I could rest and contemplate (and also didn't have to worry about that friggin icy stethoscope. Really, what do they do, keep them on ice? It really can't be too healthy to have someone jabbing at you with a cold bit of metal.). I ran over the rest of the day before in my head.

Within ten minutes there were a whole crap load of cops and paramedics swarming all over the warehouse. Jack was finally dead, and as it turned out my bullet (the first one, the head shot) ricocheted off his skull at an angle large enough for it to skirt the head, never truly penetrating to the brain. They found enough of his head to verify that the bullet had made a groove in the skull. I guess that's good.

Anyway, Jack was dead, and so was Harv. It was incredibly hard for me to believe that Harv had sold me out like that, but money is a great debater, and Harv was never one to quibble over something as unimportant as loyalty when money was philosophizing. When the cops cracked open the rest of the boxes, they found a large number of the more illegal forms of firearms, very nearly enough armaments to equip a small army.

Jack had been ready for anything, apparently. I just couldn't figure out why he had tried to kill me. The odds of my being able to stop him alone were quite small, and the only person who could possibly have helped me was the captain. Thinking of the captain gave me a queasy feeling, and I remembered he hadn't been there when I was loaded into the ambulance. In fact, I hadn't seen him at all since I left the office.

The more I thought about it, the more worried I got. If Jack could try and kill me, then what was to stop him from going after the captain? In fact, how did I know that he hadn't gotten the captain? Suddenly I didn't want to be alone. I reached over and pushed the call button. Almost immediately a peppy little nurse with frizzy blonde hair poked her head in the room.

"Well good morning, sleepy head!" Her voice grated on my nerves like fingernails on a chalkboard, although I guess most guys would have found it quite nice. Of course, most guys will call anything nice as long as everything below the neck is in the right proportions. She pulled back and I could hear her call to the doctor, and I was able to determine that the proportions were quite nice. Maybe her voice wasn't so bad after all. "You've been asleep for a while."

"Have I?"

"Yup." She busied herself with taking my blood pressure, slinging the cuff around my upper arm and pressing that friggin icy stethoscope on my inner arm. She grasped the knob and started pumping (and that's not a metaphor, you sick perverts).

"Am I alright?" She eyed me suspiciously, her pumping hand frozen in mid pump.

"How do you mean?"

"Am I going to live?"

"Oh." She gave a little laugh and her face lightened up quite a bit. "Yea, you'll be fine. Just a little banged up. We had to stitch where you got the knife and the bullet, but all in all you got lucky." She went back to the pumping, causing the cuff to tighten until it felt like my forearm was going to pop off. She released the catch and, with a soft wheezing sound, the cuff loosened. I glanced up as the doctor strode in.

"Hey John."

"Hey Doc."

"Listen, John, I gotta tell ya. I'm glad you want to help me out and all, but I can assure I got all the practice I need in med school." It took me a second to realize he was trying to be funny.

"Ahh. Good one." I felt a little white lie wouldn't kill me, and it certainly seemed to make him happy. Course, I don't think he'll be the next Carrot Top, but that isn't necessarily a bad thing. The nurse had moved on to temperature, and had one of those little ear guns poised next to my right ear. She jabbed it in and the sudden coolness on my inner ear tickled.

The doctor glanced down at the chart, and then nodded. "Well, John, I think you're gonna be ok. Nothing overly serious. We put fourteen stitches in you, six for the knife and eight for the bullet. We actually have the bullet, if you want it." I wasn't too sure I did. I mean, that little hunk of metal had been buried in my body. If I wanted stuff that came out of me, I'd walk around with a doggy bag for every time I thought I was gonna hurl.

"The rib is gonna be fine, but only if you actually listen to me this time and stay off your feet for a few days. Rest, boy, rest." I nodded, or tried to. It's tough to nod when there's a large instrument sticking out of your ear. The nurse read my temperature aloud and removed the device, walking over to the doctor and scribbling down the number.

She then winked at me and headed off, swinging her hips as she went. The doctor's eyes followed her out, and then turned to me. I could tell that his somewhat advanced years had done nothing to his ability to appreciate proportions. "Man would I like to hit that..." He shook his head and looked dejected, then seemed to realize I was still there.

"Right. Ok, you need rest, so there's no way I'm letting you out of here today." He started for the door, and then turned again. "By the way, you have two visitors. You up to seeing them?" I nodded, finding it much easier now that there was nothing trying to root its way into my brain, and he left.

Two visitors. I was suddenly a popular guy. A brush with death tends to do that, I guess. The first one walked in a few seconds later, and I smiled. "Miss Emily!"

She blushed. "Hi John."

She sat on the corner of the bed. "I can't stay long. I just wanted to let you know that I'm worried about you."

"Thanks."

"No problem." She told me how she had gone to my apartment at 6:30 and, failing to find me there, had looked everywhere for me. I got a crazy mental picture of her standing in my living room, looking perplexed, then turning over a couch cushion and being surprised when I failed to appear. When my lip started hurting (from biting down to keep from laughing), I let the image fade.

"It wasn't until I saw the news that I found out where you were. Why did you leave?" I recounted the story to her, and then found myself staring deep into her eyes. A guy's gotta be careful around eyes like that. If you don't watch out, they'll suck you in and never let you go. The urge to be careful was quickly fading away, though, and I wasn't upset in the least. "I was worried about you," she said. "Don't scare me like that."

"I won't. I promise." She leaned down a little, and I stretched up a little, and this time there was no doctor to interfere. Once, when I was a kid, I went to the park on the Fourth and watched the fireworks. They were amazing, colorful and loud and just plain out spectacular. It was an experience that I never forgot. Of course, that has nothing to do with what happened then, but I'm not going to tell you about that, so get over it.

"I gotta get going. I'll stop by later, ok?"

"Alright. I'll be waiting." She smiled and, I could swear, blushed just a little, then headed out. I sat there, filled with bliss and practically floating, and so didn't notice when my next visitor came in until he spoke.

"Hello John."

"Captain? Oh, thank god. I thought something musta happened to you." He nodded gravely, shut the door, then walked over to the windows, the ones that looked out into the hall, and slowly shut the blinds. "Captain?"

"Secrecy, son. Secrecy." He raised one of the blinds and glanced from the left to the right and then dropped the blind back in place. "Good job getting Jack, by the way." He strode over to the other side of the bed and looked at me. "The problem is that we know for a fact his network had to have been quite large, and we're more than a little worried about retaliation."

As if to emphasize the point, he jerked his head toward the door. Someone (my guess is the proportionate nurse) had knocked a pan or something over, causing a loud clattering. When nothing happened for a little bit, he continued. "There were a lot of guns there. We're also afraid someone high up might be involved."

"High up?"

"Yea. We found Roscoe. Well, his head anyway. We aren't really sure where the rest of him is." He shook his head, probably in an attempt to clear the image of Roscoe's dislocated head from his mind. "The problem is that Roscoe was still supposed to be in the holding cell. We hadn't released him yet."

It took me a few seconds to realize what he was saying. "Wait, so you think there's a mole in the station?" He nodded. "Aww man."

"Yea, bad news, huh?"

"Very." I looked down the bed, toward where my toes were pushing the bottom of the blanket into two distinct tents, and tried to think. Unfortunately, the slowly forming headache I had refused to acknowledge earlier was getting a little upset with being ignored, and so had taken to throbbing rhythmically like some insane back up dancer at a pop concert. I looked back at the captain, silhouetted in the sun shining through the window, and again noticed how old he looked.

"How've you been, Captain? I mean, seriously. You seem like you're having some bad times." He lowered his head, slowly.

"John, they're forcing me out." I got the impression that he had been prepared for this, possibly even made cards to study from.

"What?"

"They're forcing me out. They had already decided I was a bit old to be in charge before all this happened, and now... well..." He didn't need to finish. They took the recent events to be a reflection of his declining effectiveness. "You know what's the worst, John?" I didn't, but I was pretty sure he was going to enlighten me so I didn't say anything.

"The worst is being told that you're just too old to keep doing what you love." Good ol' Captain. Never let me down. "The worst is when the aristocracy you've worked all your life to help suddenly decides you're of no more use to them and tries to shunt you off. That's the worst."

I listened, not quite comprehending, as he continued. "The worst is when they force you into retirement and then make you pick your own friggin replacement." He lowered his head again. "Aging sucks, John. It does something to you."

"They're forcing you out? How can they do that? You've been nothing but good for them." In some cases you would only say something like that when you were trying to convince someone the truth wasn't really the truth, but this wasn't one of those. The captain really had been nothing but good for The King's Men, and this news really was terrible.

"I know that. And I have a sneaking suspicion that they know that too. But you know politics, John." Actually I didn't, but I nodded anyway. "The King is above it all, but all us lowly civil servants... We serve the will of the people, John. The people above us have their own necks to consider, and when it comes right down to it that's all that matters to them. Nobody seems to care that they're pushing out an old man whose only real problem was loving his country too much."

"Oh man. I'm sorry, Captain."

"Don't be. It had to happen one day." He smiled. "I'm just blowing off steam. When you can't let it go sometimes you end up doing some odd things." He stopped and stared off out the windows on the other side of the room, the ones that opened to a spectacular view of the concrete wall of the building next door. "You were my pick, by the way."

"You mean, to replace you?"

"Yea. I picked you, and they liked it, so I was supposed to ease you in, show you some of the inside tricks. I picked you 'cause you were perceptive, John. So friggin perceptive..."

I couldn't think of any words to say. "You know, Dumpty was perceptive too. He wasn't quite as bright as some of the other guys, but he was someone you could count on when the going got tough. Plus his luck was just crap." I had to agree with that one. Dumpty had never been an incredibly lucky guy, and his little tumble over the edge just proved it. "It's too bad, really. A few more seconds and he'd still be alive." Whoa.

"Wait. What?"

"Dumpty. If he had gotten there a few seconds later he'd still be alive."

"What are you saying, Captain?"

"Oh, didn't you figure it out yet?" He turned from his contemplation of the wall and walked to the side of the bed. "I thought you were better than that." I heard a little popping sound as he used his foot to pull the bed plug, effectively cutting off the nurse call. "I killed him."

* * *

The news hit me like a bomb. The captain had killed Dumpty? What? I ran through things in my head. Why would the captain kill Dumpty? He just said he liked the poor guy, and I believed him. Why, then? Unless... Unless he had seen something. But, what could Dumpty have possibly seen that would have made the captain kill him?

That's when it hit me. The captain's anger at the government that had apparently rejected him, the fact that the King's visit this year would be the last the captain was in charge of, Jack's sudden appearance... "You were Jack's backer."

The captain chuckled. "Maybe I didn't overestimate you after all."

"But where'd you get the money?"

"Oh, please. I've been playing the stock market for a long time, building up my retirement fund. All that social security crap is just a crock. By the time I actually need any of the money they forced me to put away, it'll be all tied up in some senator's private yacht. I knew this day would come, and I figured that as long as I was going, I might as well take someone with me."

"But, why? You've been all about law and order your entire life. What would make you change now?"

"I told you. Time changes people." He reached into his coat pocket and pulled out a needle. "And now time is gonna change you." He grabbed my arm and I suddenly knew I had to keep him talking.

"Wait."

"What?" He pulled the plunger on the needle.

"Can you please just tell me why Jack tried to kill me yesterday?"

"Oh, that's easy." He pulled back, succumbing to the one flaw I knew I could count on: the captain loved to tell war stories. "I told him to."

"But why?"

"Because you knew about the plan with Ricky. It was all set, too. Do you realize how hard that was to set up? Seriously. Ricky was a terrible actor, so we couldn't very well ask him to do what we wanted. We had to set him up, get a guy to go and buy off him right when we knew you'd be headed back, and then make sure he didn't know the truth, just our version of it."

"Wait, then why'd you kill Swanson and Martell?"

"Confusion, my boy. Confusion." So I had been right that far. "It was perfect! I was going to be able to put a tiny number of men on the King and shunt the rest off on a wild goose chase." He looked wistful again, then chuckled. "But no, you had to figure that part out."

He was leaning over again, holding the syringe out so I could see it. "This little baby is gonna make you have a heart attack, ok?"

"How are you gonna get away?"

"Who said I am?" He opened his coat and showed me another needle. "The shock is gonna kill me too. I'm just too old, John. The station is my life, and when they take it away then what'll I have left? This would have been my crowning achievement." He flicked at the needle with his finger, and it made me think of the absurdity of sterilizing the needles used for lethal injections.

"So why even bother killing me?" I was panicking, and I think he knew it.

"Come now, John. Even you should be able to figure that one out." I thought about it and suddenly realized he was right. I had foiled his plans, albeit through dumb luck, and now he was taking it all out on me.

"I'm the government now."

"Bingo." He touched his nose.

I started to sit up and quick as a flash he was on my chest, sitting there and grinning at me. "Betcha thought I didn't think of that, huh?" I couldn't move my upper body, and my arms were trapped against my sides. For an old guy he was pretty strong.

He lowered the needle and I caught a glint of light in his eyes. It gave him a definite maniacal look. That's when I realized that he really was a maniac, and that knowledge apparently let a bit of adrenaline into my system, because the next thing I knew he was flying off the bed, and I was on my feet staring down at him.

He looked up at me, glaring, and muttered something that I didn't quite catch. "What?"

"I said it never friggin ends. You're supposed to die."

"Well, I'm sorry. I just don't see that happening." He hung his head, then started struggling to his feet.

"Little help here?"

"How dumb do you think I am?"

"Crud." He got himself to his feet finally and looked me in the eyes. "Don't judge me, John. You have no idea what this is like. No idea how it feels."

"I know it's wrong to do what you tried to do."

"But don't you see? It's not my fault. It's theirs. The system, John, the system. You spend your whole life protecting it and when they decide you're too old they give you the boot. It isn't fair, John. It isn't fair." He had hung his head again.

"I know it isn't fair. That still doesn't make it right." When he looked up, the light was gone. The old captain was back. He was on the verge of tears.

"John? John, is this really hapenning? Please tell me this isn't real, John." I just shook my head, sadly. He nodded, biting his lip. "Alright." He sighed, dropped his shoulders. "Goodbye, John."

I stared in horror as he stabbed the needle into his arm and depressed the plunger. As I called out for a doctor, the captain's eyes rolled back into his head and he fell forward into my arms. I sank to my knees, cradling him in my arms. His breathing was ragged and I knew he was about to die.

"John." I leaned in to listen, and as the doctors came running into the room I caught the captain's last words: "I am so sorry, John. I am so sorry."

Epilogue

I sat back. The cop, whose name was Ron, nodded and flicked the machine off. "Thanks. That should be about it." I was glad. I had told the story from the beginning, leaving out only what I saw as the more mundane bits, and only fibbing a couple of times, so I was proud of myself. I've often said that if I was meant to make up stories then I woulda been a politician, but I thought that I had told a pretty good one.

The cop packed the machine away and stood. "Sir, I'd just like to say that what you've been through, well…" I nodded slowly. "Well, I think what you were able to do is amazing. There aren't many people who could have survived all that, and, well, it makes me proud to be serving under you."

"Thank you." I had been promoted to the captain's place in the interim, until they found someone to take his place permanently. The officer nodded, then stood and walked out the door. One of the nurses came in then and asked if everything was ok. After promising her that I would call if I needed anything (Jell-O, maybe), she left, turning off the lights and shutting the door behind her. Then I was alone, alone with the hum of the machines, the soft semi-darkness of dusk, and my own deep thoughts.

I mulled through all that had happened in my head, the truth and the fiction, and made sure once again that they lined up pretty well. It was from long experience that I knew there was always at least one mistake in a criminal's story, and so I had made sure I covered my tracks well. There was one deliberate clue, though.

The captain never had a picture of himself playing the trumpet, least of all in his office. I threw that in because I wanted to see if they would catch it. More importantly, I wanted to see if they could catch me.

The rest was mainly true. I had killed Jack, and Jack had killed Roscoe and the others. It was pretty nifty, actually, because now I wouldn't have to pay him. He had wanted a lot of money, but now I could use all that cash to leave the country after it went down. Maybe go live in Africa. I do love elephants... Maybe I'd even take Miss Emily with me. If she'd go with me, of course. I'm not a bad guy. Really.

All that stuff about the captain and his retirement, that was only partially true. I knew that the captain was being forced out, and I knew that he was trying to get me installed as his successor. That was actually the key to the whole thing, the perfect motive for my invented crime. I smiled to myself in the dark. Now it was all set. The main shipment of weapons had been sent to the warehouse, but one small box was sent to the other side of Breco. We didn't really need that many guns, especially since the last box had all the best stuff.

The plan was to let the rest of the force think they had stopped the plan so they just wouldn't be prepared for when the real deal went down. I reflected on my own genius as I thought of how I had them all watching the King. It gave me the perfect opportunity to get at my real target, the King's head of security, Mike Rizzoli. Mike was a distant relative of the King's and had apparently used his influence, however remote, to get himself a job with the King despite his rather checkered past. Apparently he was quite adept at what he did, because he had risen quickly, less than five years and he was already in charge of all security measures, including getting the assistance of local law. Of letting us know exactly where they'd be, and when. It was perfect. I even knew exactly where the security would be the most lax.

I could still remember when I first met Mike, at the trial, and the smile he had flashed at the three of us. The smile that said he had done what he was accused of, what he had enjoyed doing. He got away with killing my brother, but if I had my choice, he wouldn't get away this time. No sir. Not this time. This time he would pay. I fell asleep smiling a real smile, the first one in a long time, thinking of the King's visit.

The End
Fin
No More
Adieu

Printed in the United States
1439200001B/99